She

Kelly Keefe

She

Vanguard Press

VANGUARD PAPERBACK

© Copyright 2025
Kelly Keefe

The right of Kelly Keefe to be identified as author of this work has been asserted by her in accordance with the Copyright, Designs and Patents Act 1988.

All Rights Reserved

No reproduction, copy or transmission of this publication may be made without written permission.
No paragraph of this publication may be reproduced, copied or transmitted save with the written permission of the publisher, or in accordance with the provisions of the Copyright Act 1956 (as amended).

Any person who commits any unauthorised act in relation to this publication may be liable to criminal prosecution and civil claims for damages.

A CIP catalogue record for this title is available from the British Library.

ISBN 978-1-80016-533-5

This is a work of fiction. Names, characters, businesses, places, events and incidents are either the products of the author's imagination or used in a fictitious manner. Any resemblance to actual persons, living or dead, or actual events is purely coincidental.

Vanguard Press is an imprint of
Pegasus Elliot Mackenzie Publishers Ltd.
www.pegasuspublishers.com
First Published in 2025

Vanguard Press
Sheraton House Castle Park
Cambridge England

Printed & Bound in Great Britain

Christina –

This book is dedicated to all my relations. Especially my teachers who have supported me along my journey of remembering and embracing my truest and most expressed self. I'd also like to dedicate this book to every woman in the world who is in their power, fighting for their power, and/or rising into their power. May we all continue to remember.

Thank you for being you! Your light is so special. Stay you.

♡

Christine-

Thank you for being you!
Your light is so special.
Stay you.

The biggest of thank yous to those of you who have always trusted me as much as I trust me to follow my dreams and march to the beat of my heart. Thank you to the dreamers, doers, and magical beings I am blessed to call friends, teachers, allies, and co-creators.

You know who you are. And there are no words to express my love and appreciation for you.

1

"Sushi?" she asked herself what she is in the mood for observing a lively conversation internally. "Eh, I had sushi twice this week. Indian? Indian gives us heartburn, don't be silly".

"Meatballs?"

"Now I am just being absurd – when is the last time we ate meatballs?".

Another lap around the market, with nothing but louder hunger pangs. Sitting at a table she decides to try to collect her thoughts. Maybe if she tries to incorporate some of those breathing techniques that yoga chick was rambling on about in her yoga class last week, clarity would come to her. After a few deep breaths, she found herself laughing softly to herself at the absurdity of her indecision.

After a couple of minutes of breathing with her eyes closed: no clarity. Surrendering on the entire mission, she chooses to go walk around the square and have something call out to her. On her way out, she heard a deep masculine voice that rushed through her body.

"Free samples. You want some. I promise," he said.

She looked over her shoulder and saw him standing behind the table filling plastic ramekins of hummus and ripping pieces of pita apart. Amused at the aggression he was applying to the pita, she laughs at how perfectly it articulates how she was feeling inside. He wasn't the most attractive man she had ever seen. He was actually oddly average. So average looking that it was intriguing. It was his voice that hooked her in though. She decided to turn his way and try a sample. After all, she was hungry, liked pita, and it was free.

"It's all natural. Four different kinds. I'm only supposed to let you try one, but I'm feeling devilish today. You can try two," she hears approaching the table.

"Oh wow, what a gentleman. Thanks," she responded grabbing two plastic ramekins and a handful of pita.

"If I had a dollar for every time that I have been called a gentleman…" He stared up to give the illusion that he was counting in his mind. "…I would have, like, twenty-three bucks if I had to guess."

She didn't want to laugh, but she couldn't help but find him amusing. He appreciated her reaction and took it as his foot in the door.

"So, I uh, I'm Mike, and uh, this is my hummus business… do you like hummus?" he said awkwardly. She could tell he was a little nervous. She found it adorable.

"I don't mean to be rude, but I mean, I did decide to come over, and I did just eat two different kinds of hummus."

"Well, yes. I suppose I could have made that assumption. But I thought maybe you just knew you were supposed to come over and introduce yourself and took one for the team trying my hummus to start this conversation."

She looked at him with both surprise and flattery. He was a bold man, and she liked it. There was something about his voice she couldn't get enough of. It was smooth; the tonality was deep and rounded out. He had one of those voices she felt confident in saying she could easily listen to all night. Before he could finish his sentence asking her out to dinner, she found herself nodding in agreement.

2

"Your journey has been so random yet somehow all makes perfect sense," she responded to his story with deep eye contact.

They were out to dinner at El Pez two nights later. Over margaritas they shared typical first date chatter. Mike revealed that he had started his hummus business three years ago, after serving six years in the air force as a pilot. He didn't think he would ever start his own company, but during his time in Kuwait, he experienced a restaurant that had a chocolate hummus which had completely rocked his world. It was at that moment he decided that one day he would own a hummus business and he would create a hummus that trumped what had blessed his palate. Turned on by his focus, drive and success, she was pleased with herself for saying yes to this man. She learned he came from a small family and grew up in South Carolina, which explained his easy-going and laid-back demeanor.

"Oh man, I have been talking so much already. I'm sorry! Enough about me… tell me about you," Mike said tilting his margarita towards her.

She started speaking slowly. Talking about herself has never been her strong suit, especially when following up a story as interesting and impressive as he had just so effortlessly done. Looking down at her drink tracing the rim of her glass with her middle finger... *Maybe if I move in a way that distracts him and potentially turns him on, I can draw less attention to needing to share about myself*, she thought.

She told him about the couple acre farm that she grew up on in Tennessee, where she was one of six children to her parents who were those crazy religious folk, as she put it. She shared how she spent most of her days after school tending to the land and would escape to Nashville every opportunity she got.

He enjoyed watching her facial expressions while sharing a story about her first time sneaking out and getting on the bus that would get her to the city (a three-hour journey).

She allowed herself to get lost in sharing what she loved about Nashville and a story about the time she ran into Russel Brand at a bar, and it was the best moment of her life to date. She regretted saying it was the best moment of her life the moment she said it, but at the same time, she knew it was true.

Before he could slip in a question, she offered what brought her to Denver five years ago. It had been a relationship with a man whom she had met one night in Nashville.

"We were together for a year and then he had to move here for work, and so along I came. We stayed together for about another year and then we didn't work out. We ended amicably and he is no longer in the picture in any way so nothing to worry about there… so now tell me, what brought you to Denver, Mike…"

And just like that, she dodged any true vulnerability in the conversation. Waving her hand in the air politely as the server walked by, the two of them in unison signal that they were ready for another round.

Conversation carried on for a couple hours. Stories and laughter were exchanged consistently. As time went on, they found one another finding an effortless physical connection: their knees accidently touching in conversation, or a long lingering hand laid on the other's arm during a climax of a story or an interesting fact about the other they found could be an opportunity to touch again.

Mike picked up the check and held the door as they left. She walked a couple steps ahead of him beginning a sentence as she looked over her shoulder. He grabbed her by the wrist, pulled her into him and his hazel eyes met her green eyes as he looked deep into her. She felt like he had just pierced her soul. She knew the kiss was coming, and she wanted it more than anything in that moment. He leaned in and kissed her hard.

He pushed her up against the building and they began to make-out like a couple of teenagers. As he went to slide his hand up under her dress, she stopped him. He looked at her out of breath and started to apologize. She put her hand up to his lips to stop him from saying anything else. She took a deep breath, looked him in his eyes and said, "Take me home to your place."

3

"So my pretty, we have been seeing each other for two months now, and I am ashamed to say I still don't know what it is that you do for a living," Mike said as he looked at her across the table with the adoring look that he always gave her and which she had grown very accustomed to.

"Oh?" she said as if she didn't know that it hadn't come up yet, followed with a sip of her glass of Pinot Noir. "I'm fairly sure it has come up before, no?"

"Well I mean, I am pretty sure that I would remember if it had. And if we did, then I am just the biggest douche ever for not remembering. But I will take that title, that's fine. But I promise I won't forget again. I promise. I am all ears, lady. Lay it on me. I want to hear all about you."

This was it. This is the moment that she would either lie or tell the truth. If the latter, maybe he would run for the hills. She really liked him; she didn't want to lie—they never stuck around when she lied. She took two more gulps of her wine and took a deep breath. Mike looked at her with a lifted eyebrow, quickly concerned about what was about to follow those gulps of wine and deep breath.

"I'm not working right now."

"You're not? How come?"

With a fast-paced nervous tonality, carrying a shakiness throughout she told him, "I was doing some consulting for a firm for three years and then they lost a couple of their major clients and they had to let me go. I have had some small personal clients since, but nothing that has stuck long term. My boyfriend at the time supported me quite a bit which allowed me to take some time to do that self-exploration thing. And then the market got tough, we broke up and things got really tough for me. I went and danced for a little while... but I have my résumé out and have started interviewing with some new agencies."

"I have so many questions. So many. Let's start with where you said dancer," Mike said with a steady cadence being able to read how nervous and worked up she had just made herself.

She let out a deep exhale, "I'm a dancer... was a dancer... am... was... I was, *am* a dancer."

"Never been clearer in my life with that answer," he shared with sarcasm oozing in his tone. "Well that explains so many of those moves you have," he continued slyly lifting his eyebrows twice while taking a slow sip of his merlot keeping his eyes fixed on her the entire time.

She smiled softly and blushed. "Why thank you. I haven't been on a stage in a while, and I really don't have a desire to go back. I don't even know why I brought it up right now, I just felt I really needed to tell you." She sighed and finished the remainder of her glass of wine in one smooth sip.

Mike exhaled and collected his thoughts. "That's okay. We all have to make ends meet somehow. I mean obviously, I have been spending time with you and I am crazy about you."

With that response, she couldn't help but be taken aback. Not only did he not run, but he just confessed that he was crazy about her. She decided to take this as an opportunity to redirect and focus on the golden ticket here.

"I'm crazy about you too, Mike," she said with her eyes sparkling. She looked into his hazel eyes from across the table and ran her foot up and down his calf.

That night after they both climaxed, she lay on her stomach while he kissed up and down her back softly.

Between each soft kiss he asked her a word of a question. "Hey... can I ask a favor of you?"

"It depends," she said with a sassy tonality. "If it is getting up and making you a sandwich, the answer is no, Mister."

He laughed and bit her ass playfully. "No, it isn't. Go and make me a sandwich. What is wrong with you?" he said with another soft laugh following. "Can you promise me you won't forget your worth and how powerful you are?"

She rolled onto her back and then sat up. This had just turned into a real conversation real quick.

"Mike... I don't know if I can promise that."

He sighed and lost himself in deep contemplation of what the next words out of his mouth would be.

"I don't know if I am okay with you not working at all, especially if going back to dancing is on the table if we are together. I can give you a job in my business! You are great with people. You can handle customer service and as I grow, which we both know I am going to, we can find even more responsibility for you. We can be hummus empire partners. It will be amazing. Put those strategy consultant skills to work! I can't believe with your looks and brains you haven't been scooped up by another agency in a heartbeat."

She ignored his comments about not being hired by another company yet.

"Hummus empire partners?" she said. She appreciated where he was coming from, but they had known each other for two months. She loved being with him, and she felt like this could be the real deal, but could she make that level of commitment so soon? Customer service? Hummus empire? She let out a long sigh.

"Okay. Let's do it."

"Really?"

"Really, really."

"I love you. I really do. I can't wait to build our lives together. I have never felt this way about someone before in my life. This is it, lady. Me and you. You ready for it?"

Her eyes filled with tears. Partially because she was so happy to hear those words out of his mouth. Also because she was so afraid to let herself dive into this full force. He grabbed her head and pulled it close to his. He slowly kissed her, lay her back down on the pillow and kissed down her neck, then abdomen, and made her moan until she screamed out that she loved him too.

One Year Later...

4

"What do you mean? You can't be serious, Mike." Standing with her left hip out and arms crossed.

"You think this is easy for me? I love you. I love you so much. Which makes this a million times harder", he said with tears in his eyes.

"If you love me so much, why are you leaving?"

"I can't explain that right now. I wish I could…"

"Oh. You could. Let me show you how easy it could be. You open your mouth, and start speaking telling me what is going on a why. See! It is that easy, Mike! Your turn".

Mike sighed and let a tear go down his cheek. "I'm so sorry. I will always love you," he said walking over to her, kissing her on the forehead. With tears streaming down both their faces, Mike put on his baseball hat, took one last look at what was his partner in life and business, and walked out the door.

Sitting on the floor of her apartment staring at the door that he just walked out of, never to return again.

From the moment the door closed behind him, she knew that this was first day of her life... again.

Her mind racing with the thoughts picking up with a momentum she didn't know her mind was capable of operating at. She was not ready for such a dramatic change like this. What was she going to do now? This was not a part of her plan. The conversation was not supposed to go this way. She was expecting a conversation about the rest of their lives, how perfect they are together and how they both have never felt so complete. And just like that... he vanished. Poof. Gone. The end.

Walking slowly around the apartment, she found herself staring for long periods of time. There was a level of numb that had taken over her entire being. Tears were not able to formulate quite yet. She knew those would surface later when the shock factor had worn off. It had only been a little over a year, but she really thought she had it this time.

The last time this happened, at least she saw it coming. Mike hadn't acted strange at all lately. They had just had sex this morning before he headed off to the office. Flash backs to memories shared in bed together filled her heart as anger and confusion coursed through her body.

Was it someone else? Was it something I did? She accepted that these were questions that she would never know the answer to. The strangest part about him leaving today, even though he just abruptly ended things and was walking out on what they have started to build over this past year… was that she still believed him when he said that he loved her.

Sinking into the couch she ordered some Chinese food while wearing her favorite sweatpants and hoodie. With waves of emotions and feeling the shock of everything, she grabbed her phone and texted Casey.

"I'm sorry I haven't been around in a while. I miss you and could really use my best friend".

Every couple of minutes she checked her phone for a text from her best friend or Mike saying this was all a big joke and he made a mistake. After thirty minutes of hawking the screen with no response, she found the tears that had been hiding all day pouring out.

5

$\mathcal{T}$he sound of the alarm clock shook her awake from a dream that felt so real. She shook her head to come back to reality. Sitting on the edge of the bed her feet softly landing on the ground one at a time as she elongated her spine and took a deep inhale in through her nose as her arms reached to the sky. She held the deep stretch and smiled into the sunshine beating down through the windows…Coaching herself, she sang out loud, "a new day to learn who the fuck I am, once again", with a sigh continued her self-coaching, "and it is now time to move on to the next chapter".

    She walked out onto the balcony and took a deep breath of the Denver mountain line. She kept her eyes closed and let the warm sun beat down on her face, as she tried to calm her mind enough to be able to make a game plan for the day. A siren off in the distance got louder and whizzed by. It broke her train of thought, which she embraced with gratitude. She looked down at her feet and decided a pedicure was on the list for the day. As she walked back inside, she noticed one of Mike's T-shirts was sticking out from under the bed.

"That douchebag still has stuff here, doesn't he?" she said out loud. She walked over to the bed, bent down, grabbed the shirt, and even though she told her self not to, from the moment she reached for it, she lost all self-control and had to put the shirt up to her face and smell it. All it took was the one sniff of the Chanel Bleu that just smells so damn good to bring her to tears.

Goddamn you Mike and your Chanel Bleu cologne, she thought as she let some tears go.

After doing a lap of the apartment with tears streaming down her face, she decided that she was going to make the decision to be over it, right there. She walked back out to the balcony and threw Mike's 'Crypto Is Real' T-shirt over the balcony to now belong to a bum or the bottom of a tire. Even when they were together and in love, she hated this T-shirt, so she was elated to remove it from her apartment and life forever. With her hair in a messy bun, she made her way into the kitchen to get lost in the making of her breakfast. After scoping out the fridge, she pulled out the ingredients to make a salmon eggs benedict, her favorite. She turned on the Beyoncé Spotify playlist and began making her hollandaise sauce in her underwear and tank top.

Cooking always makes her feel better. Her mother taught her how to cook when she was growing up in Tennessee. Every Saturday morning (before heading out for the bus to Nashville), her mom would make a breakfast spread for the family that still to this day makes her salivate just at the thought of it. Momma could cook. She still remembered the first time her mom taught her how to make eggs benedict. She was eight, sitting at the kitchen table rambling on about how Zachary, her second oldest brother, had told her that at school this week he learned that the Apollo team's footprints on the moon will remain there for at least 100 million years. As she was about to dive into a follow-up question to this fact, mom interjected with a question of her own.

"Hey, what do you say you come over here and help me make breakfast this week?"

Stopped in mid-word, she couldn't believe what she just heard.

No one is ever allowed to help Mom make breakfast, especially on Saturdays, she thought. But before her mother could take back the offer, she stopped swinging her legs back and forth and hopped out of her seat to have her feet hit the ground again. Butterflies began to dance in her stomach as she got close. This innate nervousness has always been with her. She did a twirl and slid her way over to her mom's side doing everything in her power to subdue the nerves and transform them into excitement.

With mom's guidance, together they made the hollandaise, and prepped the plates.

"And that my dear, is how you prepare the perfect poached egg," her mom said as they laid the egg on top of the bread.

"I got it!" she squealed with pride of her new skills, "please may I do the bacon too mom?"

"Not a chance, dear. That is a part of this that you will have to earn with age."

She didn't fight it; she never told anyone, but bacon freaked her out a little bit for some reason. She fell in love with cooking that day, and she spent numerous hours along side her mother learning how to navigate her way around a kitchen.

Recalling that memory for her young years before boys were of interested to her, she plated her salmon eggs benedict with intention. She poured her second cup of coffee, walked over to the table near her floor-to-ceiling windows running along the balcony, and got herself settled in with her iPad propped up on the table. She smiled with the utmost content as she her perfectly poached egg flowed out over the spinach and 'Irreplaceable' came on through the speakers.

"I'm gonna be okay," she said out loud with her fork filled with the perfect combination of salmon, egg, spinach, and English muffin raised to her mouth.

6

"*P*lanning to travel?" the attractive young man asked as he scanned the barcode of the world map and put it in the bag.

"Something like that…" she replied aloofly.

"Where are you heading? You know, we have specific region maps… might be more helpful," he said. He was trying to strike up conversation and play the hero; she could tell. He didn't get the hint by her wearing her baseball cap and sunglasses inside that she wasn't in the mood to mix and mingle.

"I don't know where I am going yet. That's the point of the map. To help me determine that," she replied sharply.

"If you don't know where you're going, any road will take you there…"

She raised her chin up a bit and felt her energy lift immediately at the *Alice in Wonderland* reference. It had always been her favorite book.

"*Alice in Wonderland*… nice."

His body language revealed his excitement thinking he just landed points and had found his in.

She readjusted her baseball hat to lower the brim and searched through her oversized bag for her headphones to give the hint that she was not budging from cool bitch mode today. She was one of those women who, even when she goes out looking 'a mess', she still looks beautiful and well put together. *Where are those damn headphones?* She ran her arm from one side of the bag to the other as if they were going to magically appear on the sixth or seventh time of doing this motion.

"Yes, *Alice in Wonderland*! I'm so glad you got the reference. A lot of my guy friends make fun of me for reading a lot and enjoying it…"

"Mmm…" she said to be respectful by trying to give the hint that she was not interested in holding conversation.

"So listen… I hope I'm not being too bold, but I'm Zane (she already knew this. It was on his nametag), and I would love to take you out some time, we could ya know, talk about books and stuff…"

She let out a soft sigh. "I have a boyfriend."

"Oh, I should have known. No worries. Have a great day," he said as he handed her the bag.

"You too. Thanks." grateful to have the sunglasses on so he couldn't see her eyes tearing up behind the shades. She didn't want to cry. She didn't want to feel anything.

On her way home she made a pit stop at Casey's place. She was hoping that she was home but knew that it was unlikely—she never was home, especially on a Thursday. But for some reason she had a feeling today just might be the day. She stopped by and pressed the buzzer for an obnoxiously long time waiting for her to pick up. No luck.

She headed back towards her apartment, with her gaze fixated on her screen while she sent Casey a text to let her know she had come by and that things with Mike were over.

She didn't have too many friends in Denver. She had been there for three years now, but still hadn't made many friends, especially of the sort that she felt she could be really herself with. She definitely didn't have anyone other than Casey to go to right after a break-up. She turned her face to the sun and hummed 'Me Myself & I' by Beyonce to herself as she kept walking, holding back tears.

Back at the apartment, she walked immediately over to the corkboard and hung up the map. She was really going to do this. How was she going to make it work? She wasn't sure... but she was going to do it.

She went and grabbed the darts off the dartboard and locked in on Africa as she lost herself to the thoughts racing through her mind once again. It was decided that a move was the next logical decision. And by logical, she knew that probably meant it wasn't logical at all, but she had been in Denver for three years now, and all that she had to show for it was two failed relationships and a void that she still hadn't been able to fill.

The apartment she had found and built for herself was stunning, but she had always been confident in her taste of apartments, so finding another that satisfied her was of no concern. She decided to procrastinate the life decision dart-throwing extravaganza by putting her apartment up for subletting. *Might as well make some money off it, rather than sell it.* she assured herself while hearing the keyboard buttons clicking. Feeling a boost of confidence move through her for a moment hyping herself up about her boss lady tendencies.

After putting her apartment up for rent, two playlists, a face mask, and a half-hour text message conversation with Casey, she found herself back at the corkboard with a dart in her hand. It was decision time. Throw the dart, and where it lands... she goes. She took a deep breath, focused on the map and got her dart throwing stance positioned. Out loud softly to herself she said, "One... two..." and simultaneous to saying 'three', she threw the dart.

She walked closer to the map to see where it landed...

Cuba? I'm moving to Cuba? She looked around the apartment as if there was going to suddenly be someone there to witness where it landed. Once it hit her that there is no one there and no one even knows that she is doing this, she grabbed the dart and went back to where she had thrown it the first time and got back into her stance.

"I'm not moving to fucking Cuba," she said out loud and threw the dart again. This time the dart landed on Lebanon. She quickly realized that she was not nearly as worldly or spontaneous as this activity and pulled the dart out again. She hoped that this time around it would be somewhere that she would actually entertain the idea of going to.

Two darts later, she found the dart landed somewhere on the East Coast. Her eyebrow raised. She was thinking a bit more dramatic, but there was a level of comfort with the landing that made her open to considering wherever it said. The dart had landed perfectly on Manhattan.

New York City, eh? She sat down right where she was and stared up at the dart sticking out of the map thinking about what it would be like to live in New York. It'll be like Denver… just no mountains. Or really clean air. Or super friendly people. And it will be more expensive… hardly a difference at all. She had only been to New York once in her life so far and it was when she was twelve with her family to go see the tree at Christmas. *Do I know anything about living in New York? Do I really want to do this?* She sat down right where she was, spun around and looked out her windows to see the Denver skyline once again. *"Fuck it. I am. I do. I do want this,"* she spent the rest of the afternoon packing some items up and imagining what life will be like in New York.

Later that day, remembering it was her mom's birthday she gave her a call and shared her new news.

"You are doing what? You are moving where?"

"I'm moving to New York City, Mom. Ya know, the Big Apple."

"Yes, thank you daughter, I know what New York City is. I did bring you and your siblings there after all. One of the most frustrating trips we all took together, with all those people around and everything. Are you nuts? We like space and nature! What are you going to do for work?

And live? What are you thinking?" Her mother rattled on. She could tell that her mom was keeping her hands busy on the other side of the phone as she spoke to keep from completely losing her mind over the news.

"I hear you. I'm not completely sold on it, to be honest. But I'm going to go for it. It's time for a change. Denver just isn't doing it for me. I have been here for three years, and I haven't found what I'm looking for, Momma."

"And what exactly is it that you are looking for that you haven't found? You are twenty-five, have a successful career, a beautiful apartment... whenever I talk to you it sounds like you are having fun. Is this all over that man? You are going to pick up your life and move over a man? For Christ's sake... he was passionate about hummus. We should have all known that wasn't going to work out. There are so many men out there."

Grateful to feel laughter move through her from the hummus comment, she felt a mutual lightening up between them. It wasn't until her mother made mention of having a successful career that she remembered that she still hadn't told her that she was laid off and was working with Mike full-time with some freelance side projects here and there.

"Momma... did you just say for Christ's sake? Menopause is serving you well... look at you, getting all wild and crazy, throwing out the Lord's name in vain."

"You cut that out. I did not say that!"

"Yes you... okay. Maybe I was mistaken." She decided to pick her battles.

"It's not over a man… has Mike served as a muse for this move? I won't deny that completely. But it's just time. I am starting to look at apartments and put some word out that I am looking to move as well as a new job. There is a lot happening over in New York. I think I might be able to find a new niche. Or myself… a new niche of myself, if you will."

"You have always been the free spirit of the family, my dear. I haven't been able to stop you from doing as you wish since you were a teenager jumping on that bus and heading off to Nashville. I will always support you; I just ask you think about what you are doing before you go jumping into something so crazy like this. You hear me?"

"Yes Momma. I hear you," she said as she scrolled through another page of craigslist postings of apartments for rent.

"Mmm. I love you. Keep me posted on what you are doing and where you are."

"Will do, Momma. Oh and by the way…"

"Yes?"

"Happy birthday."

"Thank you, my lady. I knew you would get to it eventually. Be good and love yourself."

"Love you. *Ciao bella.*"

She clicked through a couple more postings and inquired about a couple of apartments that may be a good fit. It hit her that she hadn't even thought about what she was going to do for work up to that point. Her mom definitely had a point on that. She checked her bank account.

At that moment of realization, she stopped and gave herself a hug. It was only four years ago that she began to make money and start saving. It wasn't until she met Mike that she had begun to slow down and connect with herself. She had a long way to go. Her friends suggest meditation and yoga consistently to her — she just isn't good at it. "that it is just going to have to wait until I find myself a bit more to get around to all of that," she always told her friends as they invited her to classes and sent videos for meditation.

She spent the rest of the day fixing up her résumé, inquiring about apartments, and researching moving companies. This was it... she was making the move.

While going through the listings, she found one that didn't have many differentiators from the others, but something about it stood out to her that made her feel this may be the one. It read:

Looking to sublet a huge and beautiful bedroom in the east village! The sublet would begin in March and the end date is highly negotiable. The room comfortably fits a large bed, dresser, mirror, window seat, desk, and chair. Newly renovated, exposed brick, 2 large and sunny windows, and light wooden floors. There is a great closet in the room. The living room of the apartment has exposed brick and comfortably fits two couches and a kitchen table. The apartment is on Stuyvesant Street (9th and 3rd Ave), which is a hidden street in NYC filled with trees and old buildings!

"I think this is it," she said to herself. She forwarded the listing and pictures over to her sister, Veronica and brother, Anthony—the two of the five siblings who would give her honest feedback on the apartment and city rather than get caught up in the drastic life change and make the entire conversation about talking her out of it. It would begin in March. She looked down at her phone to check the date again, February 11. Two and a half weeks. At this point, she has already sold herself on the idea, might as well roll with it. Make the move before she can change her mind about it.

Responding to the ad, she said to herself "here goes nothing!" Within twelve hours, she received a response from Zai. From the email alone, she could tell that Zai was one of those women who is impressively cool and strong in her uniqueness. She introduced herself as an artist and part-time professional. She was sure to include in her email that everything she is a part of needs to radiate from her soul and core. There was something about the eloquence in which she wrote her email that reassured her that this was a woman that has a bit of the 'I am woman, hear me roar' going on inside of her—something that she lacked. Something that she wanted. *Is that what I've been lacking and looking for?* she contemplated to herself.

The apartment was shared between Zai and Benjamin—a thirty-year-old engineer, who does not like to be called Ben, it's Benjamin. From what Zai said in her email, he was quiet but social and friendly. The two of them had made some mutual friends and the apartment was very much a home for them both. They were looking for someone who is a professional, social but not a party animal, and looking to live with people to both co-exist and connect. Their last roommate had to move out suddenly for a relocation for a job that brought them out to Denver. *How ironic*, she thought. She told Zai that she was very interested and wanted to move forward as soon as possible with the credit check and securing the space.

You haven't even seen the place or the met the people through Facetime... and you are committing to living with them and in the space? Who are you woman? she thought, as she closed her laptop and got ready to begin to make piles of what was coming and what she would be leaving behind with the latest chapter of her life.

*T*wo and a *H*alf *W*eeks *L*ater...

7

She arrived to the terminal in JFK Airport, with an unread message from Zai:

Hey! So Benjamin and I are both going to be out of the apartment working when you arrive, so we will meet up with you later! The doorman, Ron, knows you are going to be arriving and I left your name with him, so just let him know who you are and that you are moving into apartment 4B. Sorry in advance for not having an elevator. You'll get used to it... maybe. Happy move-in day. With grace, Zai.

She had such a mix of emotions for the last forty-eight hours as she finished packing up her belongings in Denver and getting ready to take a leap into the unknown territory of New York City. She really didn't know if she exactly fitted into the lifestyle and feeling of New York City. The message from Zai flirtted the line of pushing her over the edge of self-doubt, and providing her a sensation of relief. To be able to enter her new home without having to socialize could be some sort of gift. *There is no point in spending time and energy figuring out what emotions I am feeling and this is all bringing forth* ran through her mind *as she* focused on the next tasks at hand letting the emotions tend to themselves.

Airports had always been a place of comfort for her. Something about the hustle and bustle of so many people heading in so many directions, all with different stories to tell, but for this glimpse of time, here they are, all together. All coexisting with a multitude of agendas happening simultaneously. Thousands of people who live and know of worlds that she knows and will never know anything about. The last time she shared this emotion with a passerby, the elder woman closed her eyes and nodded and said, "Yes, that is what we call sonder my dear." From that day, sonder had been one of her favorite words in the English dictionary.

She walked slowly and took in all the people around her: a young family trying to bribe their youngest daughter to stop crying with her choice of any snack she wanted from the food stand. An older man who looked very lonely; a group of young professional men in their twenties—about to head off for a weekend to some party city to blow some cash and pick up women if she had to guess.

At baggage claim she patiently waited for both of her large navy-blue Patagonia suitcases to come down the luggage carousel. She found it interesting the impatience of the people surrounding her. *Is this going to be what all of New York is like?* Her first bag came around after fifteen minutes or so. She watched the wide array of luggage join the others one by one on the carousel like an army of cutter ants following the leader. There was a long space between the previous ant and the rest, and soon, the luggage parade had come to an end, with her second bag left behind. Doing her best to remain calm, even though it was always very hard for her to stay calm when things do not go smoothly or according to plan when traveling (or ever), she put on her sunglasses and sat on the edge of the carousel to think.

"No sitting on the carousel, please," said the grumpy overweight security guard walking by.

She grunted and headed towards customer service after adjusting her light skinny ripped jeans, loose-fitting white T-shirt, blue-and-red flannel tied around her waist, and her Rockies baseball cap, accepting that this may be a reality right now. She stood in line behind two other people, none of whom looked any more thrilled to be in this situation than she was.

"Where you from?" the man in front of her asked as he shifted his weight from his front foot to the back foot casually bringing himself closer to her.

"Denver. I just moved here," she replied

"Why would you move here from Denver? Work?"

"No… I moved here from Denver because… it just felt right."

She could tell that he regretted his immediate reaction because he knew it would most likely offend her and make her feel insecure. He was right.

"Oh, well… good for you! Sounds very brave! I'm sure everything is happening for a reason."

"Yes, I come from a career in consulting and looking for a new opportunity here in the city. I am confident it is all going to work out for the best," she said with a tonality that didn't match the confidence she was speaking about. "How about yourself? Where are you from?"

"Oh me? I'm from the city. I just landed from Japan. Was out there for three weeks for business. Doing a bit of consulting work myself."

Impulsively, she found herself shoot a glance over at his left hand to check for a ring. No ring. Single. A potential love affair? She shook her head softly to herself to snap out of the hopeless romantic mindset that she promised to leave packed away with her belongings in Denver. *Just have a friendly conversation and cut it off.*

They continued to make small talk while the disgruntled woman ahead of them finished up with the man behind the counter who clearly was not concerned about maintaining company protocols and levels of customer service as he would take moments to answer a personal text message from time to time.

They got along nicely, which wasn't a surprise, they were both consultants and spoke with people for a living. The disgruntled woman finally moved away from the counter mumbling under her breath as she left the room.

"Hey, I'm Jordan by the way… would you like to take my number and maybe I could show you around the city a bit once you get settled in?"

He did it. He cast the line. She was new in the city and a hopeless romantic. How does she not take the bait?

"Sure, I'd like that, what's your number Jordan?" He rattled off his ten digits and she saved him in her phone as 'Jordan Airport'.

"And your name?" he said with a smile that a connection has been made.

She pointed gracefully at the counter, and said, "It's your turn... don't keep him waiting up there, and I also would really like to make it to my new apartment sooner rather than later."

A look of defeat crossed his face, accepting that he truly might not hear from her at all. He shot a sad but strong smile at her and stepped forward to have his round at it with the non-customer-centric customer service employee.

Fifteen minutes later, Jordan was walking away from the line. Before leaving he walked back over, grabbed her hand, looked her in the eyes and said, "It was a pleasure speaking with you and I hope to hear from you sooner than later... whoever you are," and kissed her hand. She replied with a smile of flattery and soaked in the moment.

After ten minutes that felt like ten hours to her, the second bag was tracked down and it turned out that it never made its way onto the plane, and it was still in Denver. *This was not the way I wanted to start this new chapter in New York. The point was to leave that all behind. Important parts of my life are now officially still in Denver!* the internal dialogue in her head shouted. Her breathing was unregulated. Taking a few deep breaths thinking of Casey from previous moments coaching her through, "deep into the belly, hold, good. And exhale. As many times as you need, baby girl, as many times as you need."

She decided to pay the extra two-hundred and fifty dollars to have the suitcase brought right to her new apartment within the next seventy-two hours so that she could make the transition swift. Handing over her credit card with a sigh and dissatisfaction, she took one more of what she called, the Casey breath. Luckily, the movers would be arriving with her bed, a couple other boxes of clothing and shoes that would have to make do until her main staple items arrived.

She called an Uber and waited outside for its arrival. Within seven minutes she was in the back seat of Raul's Honda Civic heading towards the East Village. Forty-five minutes later, she pulled up to her apartment on Stuyvesant Street, and the next chapter was to begin.

8

*T*he street looked and felt quiet, apart from the NYU flags hanging not too far in the distance. *College kids… there are going to be a lot of college kids.* There were trees lining the street, just like Zai described in her craigslist posting. She did a three-sixty scan of her street, letting it soak in for the first time that her backdrop has gone from mountains to skyscrapers. It made her feel taller yet made her feel a bit colder inside simultaneously. Raul grabbed her single suitcase from the trunk of his car and carried it up the stairs of her building. She grabbed a couple singles from her wallet and handed them off to Raul as he passed her again on his way back to the driver's seat.

She took a deep breath, rang the buzzer, and Ron, the large fit black man who would now be her new doorman, pressed the button behind his desk and let her into her home.

"Hello, Ron, I'm moving into apartment 4B. Zai told you I would be coming today. I'm…"

"Oh yes! She told me! Nice to meet you. I'm Ron," he said with a cheerful tone and put his hand out to shake hers.

"Great to meet you too!" she said with a smile to match his tone.

"Zai and Benjamin... by the way, do not call Benjamin 'Ben'; he does not like it. Take it from me. I did that one time when he had just moved in and woo, let me tell you. Just, call him Benjamin. But anyhoo, yes, Zai and Benjamin left you a key right here, so here, this is yours," he said as he put the three keys on a single key ring into the palm of her hand. "You can head on up and make yourself at home is what I was instructed to tell you from Ms Zai herself."

She picked up a soft Southern accent from Ron.

"Thank you, Ron. I really appreciate it. I noticed a slight accent. Where are you from originally?"

"Oh me? I'm originally from Mississippi, ma'am," he responded, shifting in his seat fully embracing his Southern charm now that it has been picked up on and acknowledged.

"I'm originally from Tennessee. Been out in Denver for the last three years or so. Great to meet you, Ron. The movers should be here within the next three hours or so. I don't have too many items coming along with me... I carried light and left a whole lot behind in Denver," she said in a way that her voice trailed off towards the end.

"A Tennessee girl! Welcome, welcome! I will give you a call upstairs when the movers arrive to let you know they are heading up. You let me know if you need extra hands or a bodyguard."

With a large genuine smile, she thanked him as he tipped an imaginary hat on his head and smiled.

Standing in the stairwell, she prepared to embrace the first time she would be tackling the four flights of stairs that she would conquer every time she longed for her space and a bed to rest. The stairs were short and steep. *A great way to keep me drinking responsibly in fear of a single misplacement of a foot that would end in tragedy,* she thought. By the time she hit the third floor, she was grateful that her second suitcase had been left behind; she couldn't imagine taking this trip more than once with a suitcase in her hand. With each step of the final flight, slowly moving forward one step at a time, she tossed the suitcase to have it slide across the floor to be stopped by the door of apartment 4B… her apartment.

She looked at the number and letter and placed her right hand up against the door and leaned her forehead against it. She took a couple deep breaths. *I am really here. This is my new home. I really just picked up my roots in Denver and moved to New York.* Knowing this was the first time she would be seeing the apartment other than in pictures, she said a little prayer to herself (the first time she had prayed since her childhood in Tennessee) that the apartment was going to match the pictures and that everything was going to be okay. She placed the key in the hole, turned the key… and had the wrong key. Oh cmonnn! she exclaimed to herself and she stomped one foot while choosing another key. She tried again, and this time, the lock turned, the knob released its resistance, and she swung open the door to her new home…

9

She stepped into her new home, carefully placing each foot softly while removing her baseball cap to be able to take in the space from all angles. She ran her left hand along the brick exposed wall that covered the left side of the apartment. She walked down the narrow hallway, feeling a sense of calm wash over her. She embraced it. With a few more steps, she came up to the kitchen that was to her right. It was beautiful and quaint. The gray with black accent marble countertop was aligned with her standards. Running both hands along the counter that created the remaining two walls with the L-shape they made, she smiled softly. She took in the cabinets, the double sink, and cooking tools that have already found their home in this space. This was very important to her; the kitchen is always important. There is counter space to prepare her favorite meals, although she will have to learn how to do more with less for sure. Stainless steel appliances that appear to be kept clean and in great condition filled the corners of the kitchen nooks. She caught a glimpse of green out of her peripherals and looked up to see an array of beautiful plants filling the space between the cabinets and the ceiling. For the first time since the plane had landed, she was filled with elated joy. *There is life in this space.*

Right behind the high countertop that creates the perimeter of the kitchen was a dining table surrounded with four chairs that were all very different from one another. If she had to guess, they all came from antique shops in the surrounding boroughs. The wall opposite of the brick wall was a deep red, creating a very warm feeling to the apartment. There was a fantastic wall décor placed on the wall behind the light green high-backed antique chair including three records, floating bookshelves, and an Alex Grey painting. She would have never put any of these things together. You can tell that an artist lives here.

She turned her head and took a look into what was now her living room. The long tan couch and matching love seat looked very comfortable (broken in, but not worn). They were paired with a teal papasan chair with a dark wood finish. They hugged around the kidney shaped dark wooden table that matched the papasan. There was a large TV mounted to the wall of what turned out to be Zai's room. In the far corner of the apartment there was a standing desk with a tall stool tucked neatly away in the corner. She thought she was in love. She found herself walking to every inch of the apartment and running her hands along everything. Not only was it aesthetically beautiful, but she loved the way that everything *feels*.

The wood floors were stunning. One single large light brown shag-like carpet took up a space in the common area. A standing plant stood tall taking in the sunlight shining on its shoulders. She stood alongside it and took three deep breaths allowing the warmth of the sun rays to hit her cheeks. When she opened her eyes again, she slowly turned and took in the space again from a new angle. She had hit the craigslist jackpot.

She walked around feeling various furniture for a bit and then headed towards the two of four doors that are open, assuming that they will be her bathroom and bedroom. She walked to the middle door and pushed it open. The bathroom was simple: clean and nice. She walked over to the tub and noticed that it is rather deep so a bubble bath will be plausible. *Check,* she thought. Small black and white checkered tiles cover the floor. The shower curtain, clear with red polka dots she isn't crazy about... but she isn't worried, she can tolerate it for a couple of months until she knows she has the freedom to change it. Walking out, she made her way to the other open door.

She gently pushed the door and allowed it to swing open with a softness. The first thing that caught her eye were the two tall windows at the far end of the room. One of them opens to the emergency staircase with a small platform. Perfect to take in some air and sit. Her hands ran along the sliding closet door and opens it. She reminds herself she will have to learn to do more with less, but between the closet and dresser that is on its way with the movers, it should be fine. Her walls are a clean green. A couple shades darker than the shade of grass. *I can definitely work with this* she thought.

She walks to the center of the room, slowly sits down. As if startled, quickly she pops back up and grabs her hat from the counter. Now that the full perspective was taken in, the hat can return. Back to the center of the room and without any hands, crossed her feet and brought herself to the ground. She extended her legs and lay back with her hands behind her head. She was really here. She was lying in what was now her room in the East Village of New York City. Just fourteen hours ago she was in Denver, where she lived. She wondered what time she should expect her roommates.

She grabbed the one suitcase that did make its way with her and brought it into her room. She unzipped the curves and exposed some of the pieces that make up her essence. Her favorite hoodie that read 'Russell Brand is my homeboy' and yoga pants safely made their way to the East Coast. She changed, feeling it was only right that Russell be a part of this moment with her. She walked out of her room and did a couple of twirls and slides across the wood floors of her new apartment. Opening and closing a few cabinets and at last she found where the mugs were kept. She removed a plain white matte-finished mug and filled it with filtered water that she found in the fridge. She hugged her mug and held it to her face as if she were about to blow on it. She looked around at her space; a space filled with reflections of two people she didn't know at all. Everything new and so much unknown to come to light soon with time, experience, and trust in herself.

10

*B*y seven p.m., the movers were finished bringing her furniture up the four flights of stairs and had finished putting together her bed. The room appeared a lot smaller once everything was put together. *More with less. That's the mantra. Beautiful*, she reminded herself. She pushed around a couple of boxes checking the labels she'd written in sharpie. The fourth box she spun around to reveal the contents had the bedding that she was looking for. She'd washed them and vacuum packed them right before leaving Denver, so she was hoping they would still have the fresh sheets scent. She unzipped the plastic and pulled out her fresh white linens; she wrestled with the fitted sheet and the corners of the bed, as she does every time since she was a kid. She then grabbed one side of the sheet by its corner and flipped it out into the air allowing it to softly parachute down across the queen-sized bed that she adores. As she was tucking in the right side of the bed, she heard the door at the front of the apartment open and close.

"'Ello? Anyone home?" She heard a deep man's voice call out. She paused mid-tuck as if she was caught doing something promiscuous and was trying to go incognito. She stayed perfectly still for about thirty seconds and then realized that this is the moment that she should probably say something and make sure her first encounter with Benjamin was not ridiculously awkward.

"Hey! Yes, I am in here! I will be right out!" she finally called out, with a shakiness in her voice. She didn't realize how nervous she was until she heard the tremor in her voice while tucking in her sheet and slowing down her breathing, she collected herself to be able to walk out cool, calm, and collected. As she put her hand on the doorknob, she looked down slightly and realized she was still wearing her 'Russell Brand is my homeboy' hoodie and panicked. She thought *First impressions here lady. No need for anyone to know about your Russell brand obsession quite yet*, as she ran back over to her suitcase and found a boyfriend-fit T-shirt and threw back on her ripped jeans. She swallowed the knot that had formed in her throat as she placed her hand back on the knob once again.

When she came into the common area, he wasn't in the kitchen or living room.

"Benjamin? You still here?" she called out to the empty space.

"My turn to be right out! Just changing out of these clothes," Benjamin called out from his bedroom.

As she waited, she moved to a couple of locations trying to get into a position that made her feel and look comfortable and inviting. She couldn't help but think that no matter where she was or placed herself, it was awkward. After accepting that is all probably in her head… she sat down on the love seat and allowed herself to sink into it and take in more of the wall décor and various knick-knacks that were dispersed around the apartment.

After ten minutes or so, the other black door with the old-fashioned gold knob closer to the entrance swung open and a tall, burly, handsome blond man wearing chunky black-framed glasses filled the door way. Benjamin was wearing relaxed fit dark jeans and a navy-blue T-shirt that said 'Clark Kent Was Vegan' in a salmon color. He looked right in her direction and flashed a charming and impeccably white smile her way.

"Hi there! Welcome home!" he said as he walked towards her. She stood from the couch and met him halfway with an impeccable white smile to match his as she opened her arms. She felt like she hadn't received a hug in weeks. It had only been about eighteen hours from when Casey dropped her off at the airport and they hugged and cried. Regardless, it felt as if weeks had passed already since her time in Denver. His hug was warm and strong. It felt genuine. She couldn't help but wonder if he was this kind to everyone...

It must be a vegan thing, she thought.

They both sat down in the living room, picking opposite ends of the same couch. They started small talk as Benjamin sipped on his local-brewed IPA. They delved into conversation about how her flight was, how was his day, what he does for work, and what brought her to the city. There was a really natural synergy between the two of them and she was overwhelmed with how lucky she was feeling about how smoothly everything was going.

She learned that Benjamin grew up in Salt Lake City, Utah and was raised in a Mormon family. He never felt like he fit in with his community, including his family, and questioned the religion and the way his family lived from a very young age. Most of his life he felt like an outcast. He wasn't popular in school, but he was far from unpopular. His natural good looks and athletic abilities got him a pass to parties and the girls, as he put it. Not in a pompous way at all, but in a relaxed state that showed that he is confident in who he is and is self-aware. He went to school at the University of Utah for two years against his will, but still under the control of his family in many ways. During the spring semester of his freshman year, he started to have feelings for one of his male classmates. He had never considered himself gay, but now this connection was starting to have him question everything.

Benjamin and his first male partner, Marc, experimented for the entire spring semester and decided to call things off as the summer was nearing. During that summer, Benjamin felt guilty for not sharing this with his best friends. He opened up and shared about his relationship with Marc to a childhood friend he had been friends with since they were three. Benjamin's friend broke his vow to not tell anyone, and before he knew it, the entire community had heard, and his parents were not shy in sharing their disapproval with him. His father came at him and raised both his voice and fist to Benjamin when he said he wasn't sorry and wouldn't promise that it wouldn't ever happen again. The moment his fist met

Benjamin's high cheek bone, he decided that was the moment he was going to leave Utah.

He went and finished his degree in bioengineering at Arizona State University, where he lived in Tempe for four years. He was serving tables for the first year out of school while applying to jobs all over the country. He finally got a job offer as a Biomedical Technician in Manhattan, and he had been in the city ever since. This year would mark his five-year anniversary with the city.

"You know... the funniest thing about it all really..." he said, leaning back looking at the ceiling, "I have never been with another man since Marc either. All of that happened, and I have never even kissed another man since."

She sat and looked at Benjamin with deep gratitude at how open and vulnerable he had just been with her within only an hour or so of knowing each other.

"It's a pleasure to meet you. I totally relate to you on the whole growing up feeling you didn't fit in with your environment. I grew up on a farm in Tennessee, one of six kids and parents were super religious. They pushed it on us pretty hard; I never really felt it. I would go to church kicking and screaming every week... but I went. Once I hit high school at fourteen, I would sneak off to Nashville any chance I got. My parents always called me a free spirit which I found ironic because I always felt so restricted on everything that I wanted to do with my life. I went to Belmont for—"

Benjamin interjected, "Belmont... isn't that a..."

"Catholic school? Yes. It is. Mom and Dad promised to pay for school if I would go to Belmont. I decided to take one for the team; looking back now, it really wasn't too bad, but I couldn't wait to get out of there by the end of senior year."

"Interesting. Debt free… can't fault you there. I have another four years left of my student loan debt, so good for you girlfriend," he said as he moved around and placed his feet on the ground. "I'm going to grab a beer real quick; do you want one?"

She put her chin up in the air slightly to think about if she did or not. "You know… I would love a beer. Thank you."

"You got it. Now please, continue. What did you go to school for?"

"I graduated with a marketing degree. Had no idea what I wanted to do. I figured I could end up doing something somewhat productive with that eventually. I got a job at a marketing agency right out of school and worked there for three or so years. Fell in love with a man, together for a year, and then he got relocated for work and I followed him to Denver. Things fell through with the guy I was dating, but I decided to get my own place in Colorado and see what happened. I started freelancing while I was out there and fell in love with it. A little over a year ago, I fell in love once again and that relationship was almost too easy. We broke up about three weeks ago…"

"Three weeks ago? Isn't that about the time you reached out to Zai about moving to the city? Did you move here because of that?"

"Well… yes. Well, no. Hm, yes, no?"

Benjamin took a sip of his beer and raised a single eyebrow in her direction as if he was saying that she can't fool him, but that he wasn't judging her.

"Well dear, I am glad to have you here. We needed some fresh blood in this place. The last woman who was here, she was all right… but we were not crying when she gave the news that she was going to have to hop ship."

"I appreciate that, Benjamin. It has only been all about, oh I don't know, six hours or so, but I am glad to be here too. Now tell me, where can a girl get something good to eat around here? I'm starving."

"Oh honey… it's New York City. Go have yourself a stroll and take your pick. Just avoid the sushi place four blocks over. Never go there. I repeat… Never. Go. There."

She saluted him and headed off to her room to find a jacket to put on over her T-shirt before heading out for her first adventure.

11

She walked about five blocks and went exploring for what would be her first meal out in the city. She found a cute café that looked warm and inviting.

The ambiance was warm. Dim lighting but in an inviting way. The tables were covered with gray-blue cloths and everyone there was dressed tastefully. The walls were decorated with the photography of local artists. She found herself staring at a photo from Manhattanhenge 2013. An older man sitting at the counter noticed her focused attention and decided to interject her train of thought.

"Manhattanhenge. You know what it is?"

"This is a thing? Like, this happens?"

"Oh sure! Every year, twice a year. Both occurrences fall evenly spaced between the summer solstice. End of May and mid-to-late July usually."

"It's beautiful," she said. She shook her head gently. She peeved herself anytime she stated obvious things just to have something to say and fill silence.

"That it is. Be sure to find your way to the highline when it happens. You can see it sitting perfectly on the skyline, just like this. It's one of those moments that you'll never forget and takes your breath away. And listen to me,

I am an old man. Take advantage of experiencing as many moments as you can that will take your breath away."

She gave him a soft smile and nodded her head to let him know that she was listening and soaking in his advice for both the here and now and future.

"Thank you, kindly. I will make sure that I get to experience it." They shook hands gently and with kindness and she went to find herself a seat at a table.

A small table towards the back of the restaurant was available. She took the seat that allowed her to face the door. Her father had drilled into her head at a young age to always take the seat that keeps your back from facing the door whenever possible. He had anxiety and control issues. He was always afraid that if he was not able to see a door and react immediately in the case of an emergency, he would never be able to forgive himself. He was fortunate to never have to test his theory—but it was a quirk of his that had traveled with her from Tennessee.

The cafe was small, with about twelve tables. There were cloth napkins with heavy silverware on the table she sat at. A young man came over and filled her glass of water as she began to look over the menu. It appeared she had been pulled towards a vegan café. She wasn't a vegan by any means, but she was open to exploring it—after all, she felt like the place chose her.

Her waitress, Alicia, came over with her dark brown messy bun bobbing around on the top of her head and a bubbly smile and personality to match. She pegged her as a college student. When she asked for suggestions of what is good and that she has to try, she felt maybe she had misread the impulse about this café when she responded.

"Oh man... geez, everything is so good here. But if I had to choose... well, the first thing would definitely be the hummus. It is amazing! Are you a hummus person?"

It took everything in her not to slouch down in her seat and cover her face with her menu. She couldn't believe what a knee jerk reaction she has to hummus. Hummus! Mike had ruined hummus for her forever!

"Not a fan. What else do you have?"

"Oh! Okay, sorry. Yea, I could tell that was not a good choice as soon as I said that. The Cajun seitan wrap is fantastic"

"Yep. Perfect. Cajun seitan wrap, please. Can I have an extra side of avocado with that? Oh, and a cup of peppermint tea."

Alicia responded with enthusiasm, "Great! Sure thing! I'll get that in for you right now. By the way, if you want the Wi-Fi password it is... oh God... I'm so sorry!"

Holding the menu out to Alicia, she raised her eyebrows making it clear she was confused what just happened.

"The Wi-Fi password is hummus772. I'm sorry, we are known for it!"

She couldn't help but laugh.

"It's fine. I appreciate it, thank you," she said as she grabbed her phone to connect.

While waiting for her meal, she scrolled through Tiktok and Instagram. After realizing she hadn't signed into her email since everything with the apartment was confirmed, she moved along to check her Gmail accounts.

When she logged in, she saw that her sister, Veronica, had responded to the email that she sent when she began entertaining the idea of this move. She had completely forgotten that she emailed her and Anthony. Looking back on it, she found it refreshing that she had reached out to them during that time. She hadn't reached out to any of her siblings for advice or feedback since... well, ever.

My dearest older sister,

This email found me with a level of surprise on multiple levels. Let me first say, as shocking as it was, it was more so nice to see your name pop up in my inbox. It has been quite some time since we have really talked. I think about all of you quite a bit. But anyway, you reached out asking for my opinion on you moving to New York? Big move, sis! Pretty cool, when did you get cool? You know that's my job as the younger sister to be cool. All right, again, I'm here. I promise. It's not always Veronica land (who am I kidding, yes, it is. Some things never change).

I think moving to the NYC is a fantastic idea. I don't know what you will be doing out there, but shit, anyone can find anything to do out there. Especially with the work you do... right? Is that right? Can you find work easily with the work that you do? What exactly is it that you do again?

A bit about me and what I have been up to, because I am sure your original email was partially to get that update from me too... I have been living in Thailand for the last 6 months working on a project for the magazine. Did I tell you I am working for National Geographic *now?*

Been about a year and half. It's really amazing—I can't wait to tell you all about it! Want to hear the craziest thing about all of this? Work is sending me to New York now too! I will be settling into a sublet up there in about two months or so. I don't know where about in the city I'll be since they are going to pay for it, I won't have much say.

Well, I know this is a bit delayed in response, so I don't know if you made the move or not but let me know! And if you did... I think it would only be appropriate if we got together and caught up properly. We are sisters after all.

Tell Mom I said hello and that I think about them.

Cheers,

Veronica

She couldn't believe that she had reached out to Veronica. She is a self-centered egomaniac. *What made me reach out to her?* She knew to get over that because she couldn't take it back and there was nothing she could do now — the lines of communication were open.

What are the fucking chances she is also moving to New York City? she thought as she took a sip of water and fixed her eyes on a photo of a young boy pulling on his mother's dress at a local city park. After another five minutes or so of being lost in thought, she welcomed the distraction of her wrap that came with a beautiful side salad to match. She was so hungry, and her stomach growled with excitement as the aroma of her first real meal in the city hit her nostrils.

After dinner, she re-opened her inbox to respond to Veronica's email.

Hey Veronica,

I'm glad that I reached out to you while still in Denver and that we have reconnected. I am now in the city and what are the fucking chances that you are on your way here too. Thailand, eh? Looking forward to hearing about that. We always knew you were going to be the one out of the bunch of us that would end up exploring the world for a living.

Give me a ring when you get to the city. I would really enjoy getting to see you. I could tell Mom you said hello, but I think it would mean a lot more to her if it came from you... just think about it at least, V. Let me know when you get here, my number is: 303-555-8171.

Love you always.

With a deep exhale she placed her phone in her pocket as she got up to leave. She walked with both hands deep in her jacket pockets and her chin slightly lifted taking in the city streets and her new neighborhood. She was really here. Her ignorance to her surroundings and next steps washed over her for the majority of her walk.

The news of Veronica following shortly behind her had been enough to trigger a bit of anxiety through her body. Her whole family does this to her. They always have; this was why she would escape to Nashville whenever she could... that and she loved the way live music runs through her body. It made her feel extra alive, and she is always looking for things to make her feel extra alive.

She stopped into a small-business coffee shop and ordered a small decaf coffee with almond milk. She wanted something warm in her hands to make her feel coddled and comforted. *I wish I didn't just move in a couple hours ago. I would love to ask Benjamin to cuddle. He looks like a great cuddler*, she thought. After aimlessly wandering for a couple of city blocks, she directed her wandering towards her new apartment and was ready to call it a night.

With her return, she found Benjamin had left while she was gone. She was alone in her new place once again. She wondered when Zai would be getting back; she wanted to meet her, but she was beyond drained.

In due time, such as anything, right? she thought.

She slipped back into her Russell Brand hoodie and yoga pants and did one slow lap around the apartment taking it all in. Tomorrow would be the first full day in this chapter of her life. She hadn't even been here for a full twenty-four hours and already she had made a deep connection and received news that rocked her world.

"If this is setting the tone for the city… I don't know if I am going to make it," she said to herself as she brushed her teeth and made her way to her bed that she just made a short few hours ago.

She curled up into her bed and she smiled as she cuddled in her pillows. She loves her bed. Her white sheets had kept the smell of fresh laundry thanks to the vacuum sealing, so she took in a deep breath, taking in the last of what Denver had to offer her for the time being.

12

At six thirty, the sound of her alarm clock greeted her. She has been on the same morning routine for five years now and didn't want to even think about breaking that routine. Since there was a two-hour time difference, permission for a nap that afternoon had already been granted the night before. She had grown to be very disciplined with her morning routine. She attributed her structure and discipline to her parents having her tend to the farm majority of her life.

Planting both feet on the ground, she rose and lifted her hands over her head taking a deep breath in, just as she does every morning. The sun was shining low into her windows, but it was enough for her to know it was going to be a sunny day. She made way to her door and tripped over her left boot that had fallen over down near the end of the bed. She caught herself, paused to rebalance, and with proper footing made her way to the bathroom.

She peed, brushed her teeth, and splashed her face with cold water as always. As she brought her face to meet herself in the mirror, she stared deep into her eyes for what felt like minutes. So many things unknown, and the only way for her to figure them out is to just keep moving and figure them out. She teared up while staring at herself. She released one single tear down her cheek and watched it gracefully hug the curves of her face. After wiping it with the back of her hand, she took a deep breath, and headed back to the bedroom to complete her morning routine.

By quarter to eight, she was dressed and ready for the day. She walked out into the kitchen, found herself a mug, then started a pot of water after finding the tea that Benjamin had said she could help herself to.

With a fresh cup of tea, she made her way over to the small couch and turned to face the windows to take in the sunshine that was continuing to rise and fill the apartment. Taking a few moments to be with herself, she felt that calm she had felt when walking into the apartment come to her again. She welcomed it with a soft smile and a sip of tea.

Suddenly, a wave of anxiety rushed through her, and she found herself holding tightly onto the teacup. *What the fuck am I doing here?* she thought. It hit her like the roadrunner hitting the brick wall in the old cartoons she watched growing up. *I have no plan. I don't even know people here. I miss Mike even though I am trying to tell myself that I don't, and everything is fine. What if this doesn't work out? What if I lose everything? This... this is insane... what has come over me?*

As she felt her mind beginning to take control, she heard a smooth voice hit her ears from behind her. Zai had entered the living room.

"Hello gorgeous," she said with a very cool tone and demeanor as she approached. "So nice to meet you. How was getting into the city?"

"Hi Zai! So great to meet you. Yesterday went as smooth as it could go, I think. I'm still a bit in shock that I am really here. Actually just caught me battling my mind just a minute ago."

"Girl, it's the New York City move hangover. It happens to everyone who moves here. Moving here is very different than anywhere else anyone could be coming from. You're good. I'll be right back; I need to get some tea myself," Zai said with a very comforting smile. She couldn't believe how loving and kind both Zai and Benjamin were. How did she get so lucky?

She observed Zai as she walked away. She was a very voluptuous woman with a light caramel complexion. Her hair was a gorgeous afro and very well kept. She was wearing what appeared to be a kimono, but it had a bit more flow to it. Everything about her said artist. She is just one of those people that you can tell are incredibly intelligent and creative. One of those people who keep you hanging on their every word knowing that there is great potential for the next words to be even more delicious than the last.

She was so grateful that Zai entered and broke up the intense train of thought she had been following. It really helped get her into check for a moment. *I am living in an amazing apartment with what appears to be two incredible people, and I have time to figure things out. Things are going to be okay. As long as I don't let myself lose my head; I am going to be okay.* She took a long slow sip of her peppermint tea with her eyes closed doing her best to bring her mind back to the calm clear place.

"So what are you getting yourself into today?" Zai questioned as she folded herself into a cross-legged position on the papasan chair.

"I don't know. I need to start putting my résumé out and networking so probably that…"

"Girl, it is your first day in the city! And you are going to dive right into work? Go have some fun! Go see some art… make a friend or two!"

She took another sip of her tea with her eyes closed, trying to not put a defensive wall up to Zai so soon. As she swallowed, she thought about what Zai had said, and perhaps she was right. Maybe she should take the day to go out and take in the city.

"Yea… maybe you're right. Maybe I'll do that. What are you up to today?"

"Oh my day is packed. I have rehearsal up at the studio at noon. That will probably run until three unless the director is in another one of his moods and then it'll be until five or so. And then I have a showing at a gallery up town this evening. One of my pieces is being displayed—you should come to the gallery if you're not doing anything… and I'm just going to put it out there right now. I know as of right now you aren't doing anything, so if you don't come, I know you just didn't want to."

They both laughed. Zai's sass doesn't always sit well with others, so she was relieved to see it received well. Zai continued to tell her about the production she is currently dancing in for a local theatre here in the city; they have been in rehearsal for the last three months and the showcase is to open in the next month or so.

She couldn't help but be incredibly impressed by Zai. She wasn't a very artistic person, so she always felt a bit of envy and intimidation by people who are extremely creative. As they immersed themselves in conversation, she found herself casually looking around the apartment and with every scan she found some new small detail or décor that she hadn't seen the last time.

"All right. Well, I gotta go get ready. If I'm late one more time this week, they might actually act on the threat to throw in my understudy."

"Ha, yea, definitely wouldn't want that to happen," she replied. "Oh, at some point send the address and time of the gallery tonight if you think of it."

Zai looked up from putting her mug in the sink and smiled. She grabbed her phone that was placed to her left on the counter and texted her immediately.

"No excuses. See you there." She blew her a kiss and walked gracefully into her room to get ready. Zai appeared to float when she walked. There was a sense of magic to her.

She sat with her tea overlooking the hustle and bustle of the city for another fifteen minutes or so deciding what it was that she was going to really do with herself for day. Zai had a good point. She should get an idea of where she is living and get to enjoy some life before she gets sucked back into the busy world of business. Besides, who knows who she will meet.

She got up, took a quick shower, and went into her room to see a huge pile of clothes on top of the suitcase that she has yet to unpack.

Not today. Not today, I'm sorry self, not today. Let's wait until the other suitcase that got left behind gets here and do it all together. Oh procrastination at its finest, isn't it amazing how we can justify everything and putting everything off she thought, and she shuffled through the pile looking for her black skinny jeans.

Around noon, she headed out and decided to take the subway and stop somewhere randomly uptown. As the subway flew into the terminal, the wind blew her hair back and kissed her face. She had just found her new favorite simple pleasure in life.

She got off at the Columbus Circle stop. The first thing she saw when she reached the top of the subway platform was the Shops of Colombus Circle. *Oh great, leave it to me to lead myself right to a mall. Keep it moving lady.* She walked aimlessly block to block peering into the different stores and cafes that flooded her senses every step she took. She didn't know what she was looking for. She didn't know exactly what it was she wanted to do with herself today but when she hit a book store that looked like somewhere she could get lost for a bit, she pulled open the doors and made her way in.

It was quiet. She felt she just escaped the noise and fast paced movement of the city instantly. She ran her hand along a row of books that filled the shelves of the ceiling to floor bookcases. She loved bookstores- they were filled with passion and wisdom. It took strumming her fingers along four book cases until she stopped at one and dove in to learn more of what it would entail.

It was a book of photography titled, *Men Nude*. She was drawn to it just to see what the approach of the pictures would be. It was very fascinating; it began from the 1800s and had examples of photography of men in few to no clothes and went all the way to modern times. She found herself looking over her shoulder feeling slightly uncomfortable that she had found herself drawn to and flipping through what could be perceived as soft-core porn. A man came down the row she was in, and she quickly closed the book and threw it back on to the shelf with a soft yet deep exhale of relief. He witnessed it all happen and gave her a glance with his head turned as if studying everything about her a bit more.

He was tall and had an olive complexion. He was wearing a light trench coat, pleated dress pants, and a pair of Brooks Brothers shoes. He fit the image of a successful New Yorker for sure. He took a couple steps towards her and began to look at some books on the shelf. She could tell out of the corner of his eye he was watching her to see if she moved away or if she created the space for him to step a bit closer to her.

He picked up a book, flipped through the pages, put it back in and made his way closer to her.

"Fan of photography I take it?" he said as he thumbed through a collection book by Agnes Martin.

"Yes, I appreciate the moments of life that are captured in a way that they can continue to live on. Anywhere other than the still frame of a photo, all of life is merely memories," she replied very calmly and matter-of-factly and she glanced through a new collection. Her depth shone through to the handsome man.

"Wow, I really enjoy that perspective. Very deep. You should be in the philosophy section; it's over there," he said playfully as he pointed to the other side of the store.

She turned her head to follow his finger, and replied, "Maybe I will. Great suggestion. Thanks," and began to make her way over.

Immediately she heard his voice following her footsteps.

"May I join you?"

She looked over her shoulder with a smile and nodded and tilted her head forward to signal to come on and follow her. He smiled and took a little hop and took a few quick steps to catch up to her.

13

"*I*'m Ashton, by the way," he said as they both flipped through the pages of different philosophers.

"Hey Ashton, pleasure meeting you. Book browsing is always more fun with others. Who do you have there?" she asked giving a head nod towards the book Ashton was holding in his hands.

"Plato. How clichéd, I know," he said as he flipped deeper into the book, scanned the page for a quote and then recited, "'Good people do not need laws to tell them to act responsibly, while bad people will find a way around the laws'." He lifted his eyebrows twice at her in a playful way, but it was enough to make her question her new book-browsing friend a bit. "How about yourself? Who are you holding there?"

"Neville Goddard. He is actually a favorite of one of my favorite people in the world. Are you familiar?" she said with a lightness and ease to her tonality.

"Never. What is his deal?"

"Well, his *deal* is pretty interesting. Let me see what I can remember and extract from here." Taking a moment to browse the book, she collected her thoughts. "His work came out around the 1950s—has a lot of books, video, and recordings out there. His area of focus is in the power of the imagination and how the lives we live are actually the manifestation of what we create in our imaginations. In much of his work, he elaborates on this theory that the Bible has been misunderstood and taught incorrectly over the years. God is really our subconscious, and *he* is really our consciousness, and when we follow ourselves and do right by the ultimate vision of what is best for us, we will walk in the glory of the Lord, our ultimate selves."

"Woah. That's some mind-bending stuff there. Do you study this? It sounds like you know what you are talking about."

"I have read some of his work. Most of this I know from my friend Casey telling me about it though. She's like my guru." She laughed. "I have had a couple of paradigm shifts myself while going through his work. I don't know about *really* knowing my stuff about this. If I did, then I would have multiple cars and homes by now, I think. I'm still dreaming and imagining myself on the beaches of Belize on a regular basis, and I don't see that happening anytime soon. It is aligned with the idea of the law of attraction. Are you familiar with *that?*" She didn't mean to, but she found herself finishing her sentence in a slightly condescending tone.

She could tell he was hesitant to answer her. "Maybe? I don't know. Is that what that movie *The Secret* is about or something?"

"Yep. Exactly. We can move on from this topic to something we are both familiar and a fan of… but pretty much, what we think about, we bring about., so they say."

"Got it. What I think about, I bring about. Thanks." He flipped through the pages for a little while nodding his head in a way that she wasn't sure if he was analyzing and processing what he just took in, or if he was trying to remove it from his brain.

After a minute or so, he sharply lifted his head and made eye contact with her. "Want to grab dinner tonight?"

"Ah, I have plans. Sorry I can't."

"But I thought about it!" he said as he winked at her, and they shared a laugh.

"I am going to a gallery tonight; my roommate has a piece showing. I told her I would be there; I can't miss it."

"I love art. Mind if I tag along?" he said assertively.

She didn't really have a reason to say no. She had enjoyed their time together so far, he seemed rather harmless. Besides, having someone from the city to help her navigate her way sounded pretty good to her.

"Yea, all right. I don't see why not. It starts around eight thirty tonight. It's at the Gagosian on West 21st." she said pulling out her phone knowing that the exchange of numbers was coming.

Right on cue, Ashton followed her statement with, "Here take my number and text me so I have yours. Looking forward to it. I will see you there. Let me know if you would like to grab a drink beforehand. There is a very nice place right around the corner that I really like."

She gave him a kind nod as she handed him her phone. After she sent him a text, he smiled, took her hand, kissed the top of it and told her he was very excited to pick up where they left off later.

As he walked out, she stared at the back of his head taking in everything that just happened. 'Meet people in bookstores, great place to pick up guys' were the words of wisdom that popped into her mind. Her best friend Casey back in Denver had said this. She pulled her phone out to text her a recap.

He looked back one last time as he opened the door, which allowed him to catch her still watching him too. They shared a slight smile, and he was swept up into the hustle and bustle of the concrete jungle once again.

She flipped back open The Neville Goddard collection and opened to an excerpt from Imagining Creates Reality:

Hold fast to your ideal in your imagination. Nothing can take it from you but your failure to persist in imagining the ideal realized. Imagine only such states that are of value or promise well. To attempt to change circumstances before we change our imaginal activity is to struggle against the very nature of things. There can be no outer change until there is first an imaginal change. Everything we do unaccompanied by an imaginal change is but futile readjustment of services. Imagining the wish fulfilled brings about a union with that state.

14

She decided to take Ashton up on the drink; it would make for socializing with both him and others a bit easier. They met outside Calle Dao Chelsea as Ashton told her around quarter to eight and gave each other a half-assed hug upon meeting. You could tell they hadn't known each other for very long with that hug. The pair of them looked amazing together. She wore a long-sleeved black dress that was cut in a way to expose the mid-length when walking, and thin-heeled boots. Ashton was wearing navy blue dress pants, a light blue clean pressed button down with a thin navy-blue tie, and the same brown shoes from earlier today. She ordered a glass of merlot, and he ordered a whiskey neat. She was a little turned on.

They had pleasant conversation picking back up with books to begin. From philosophy, to nonfiction, to the classics they were able to jump around and talk about their favorite works and what they have taken away from them.

"Okay. Favorite non-fiction book and why?" she said as she took a long sip of her wine.

He returned a sip of his own drink, allowed the whiskey to dance around on his tongue, and then swallowed with a slight wince suggesting that sip hit him a bit harder than he expected it to.

"George Orwell, *1984*. Hands down."

"Interesting. How come?"

He ran his hand through his deep dark brown hair, "Well, this might get a bit negative, but I think Orwell was a genius and a bit of a fortune teller. His depiction of government control over free-thought-provoking material and everyone's actions overall has been rather spot-on with some of the trends we have begun to see. I mean, I read this when I was a kid, but it was one of the few books that really captivated me, and I actually read all the way through. I was not a reader in high school. It wasn't cool. I had to be cool, ya know?" he said making sure she was still listening to him.

"I totally get it. I was an undercover reader in school."

"See, you get it. But yea, I have read *1984* two more times since school. Once in my twenties, and again recently in my thirties. And every time I read it, it is near frightening how many commonalities there are between the world he depicted and what is happening here."

"Hm… I can understand that."

"That's all you have to say in response?" he asked her, a little disappointed.

"I'm still taking it in and analyzing. It takes time for me sometimes."

"Don't analyze it. Just take it and respond."

She looked down at the ground trying to not get annoyed at this man who had known her for less that twelve hours trying to tell her how she should think and process information. He took the hint and redirected the conversation.

"So what kind of art is your roommate showing tonight?"

"You know, I have no idea. We have only lived together for a day or so, and she invited me, and I decided to go."

"You've been in the city for a day?"

"Or so…"

"Wow. Welcome to the city," he said while tipping his almost empty glass of whiskey in her direction.

"Why thank you, Ashton," she said while meeting her wine glass to his.

"Well…" he said then polished off his glass, "shall we?"

"We shall." She took three more small quick sips of her glass and reached behind to grab her jacket.

Ashton helped her put it on, which she enjoyed. They made their way around the corner to the gallery, allowing a short stent of silence to fall between them. It was comfortable.

He held the door as they entered the gallery, and they made their way towards the coat check. He took her jacket off her shoulders and put it with his and handed it to the man behind the counter. She observed and put together that it would be difficult to leave without him now, even if she decided she wanted to dip out on him at some point.

They made their way through the showcase, stopping every couple feet, to take in the various paintings and sculptures that were out on display. They would both look in silence and then one of them would prompt the other with a question or their thoughts on the piece. She was grateful that she had a companion to walk and take this in with.

In between reflection, she learned that he works in the city as a Creative Director for a Fortune 500 company. He told her about his trajectory and how he landed himself into this role about a year and half ago, and that he knows he is incredibly lucky to be able to say that he loves his job. It was refreshing to her to hear someone talk about their job and say all positive things and really love it. He then asked her what she does or will be doing here in the city.

"I have no idea… I don't have a job," she said with a tonality that she knew would catch him off guard and she found it humorous.

He stopped in his steps with both hands in his pockets and tilted his head towards her and replied, "What do you mean?"

"Well, I got laid off from my job at a consulting firm about a year ago. I did some freelance projects from there. I was working with my ex and his company up to the time we broke up. Obviously, that supplemental income went away with the break up. I decided to move here, and I am beginning to look for work now."

"Wow. That's really brave of you."

"Yea, I have to get a move on it. But I'll be fine. My résumé is strong, and the world always needs more consultants. We don't have enough of them yet," she said as she rolled her eyes at herself and let out a soft laugh.

He returned the laugh. "I'm sure you will be fine. You radiate success and beauty. You will be just fine."

She was flattered by his subtle compliment.

"Thank you, Ashton," she said paired with a smile.

"My pleasure," he replied as he continued to walk towards the next painting.

15

When they reached the second floor, she made eye contact with Zai from across the room. Zai gave her a look and a smile when seeing that she had shown up with a handsome man. She felt slightly embarrassed and got a bit concerned that Zai was going to think less of her. Just as she had that thought, she met eyes with Zai who mouthed to her "you go girl" and did two soft silent claps. They shared a smile and laugh from across the room.

Zai began to walk towards them until their paths met a mutual point.

"Hey Zai! This is Ashton. Ashton, Zai."

"Pleasure to meet you Ashton, thank you for coming out and supporting our work," Zai said as she put her hand out to shake his.

"Likewise, Zai. I always enjoy getting to immerse myself in galleries. Congratulations on being shown. Where is your piece?" he asked with a very charming demeanor.

"Let me show you both. Come this way!" Zai said with a tone that expressed flattery and excitement.

Zai led them to the far end of the second floor, where there was a roped-off section securing a sculpture that was intricate and immaculate. It made her think from the moment her eyes laid sight on it.

"Zai, this is amazing!" she said as she began to take it in.

"Aw, thank you! This is my baby. It's been in the works for just a little over a year now.

"What do you call it?" Ashton asked with his breath struggling to come out from amazement as he took it all in himself.

"What Is Time," Zai said proudly as she took a deep breath, looking at her sculpture.

"Amazing," Ashton said and nudged his beautiful date all in black and nodded to her to make sure she knew she was still his main focal point.

"Thank you, Ashton. I see someone flagging me down across the way. I'll catch up with you guys in a bit."

They smiled, nodded and went back to taking in the sculpture and Zai glided across the room in the magical fashion that she does.

It was an extra-large pocket watch that was open, and the dials and inner workings were large and elevated above the frame to be able to see the grooves of the dials. On top of the crank and dials, there was what appeared to be a sundial. The sculpture was overflowing with clocks, pocket watches, and watches that had all been melded together and arranged in a strategic randomness. Some of the clocks slightly melted and drooping—similar to the look of the work of Salvador Dali's *Persistence of Memory*. The backdrop to the intricate blending of vehicles of time, was another extra-large what she thought at first was a pocket watch. After focusing her attention to solely that piece, she came to realize that it was a compass. This compass had multiple dials that were all pointing in different directions.

She was amazed with Zai's work.

"Your roommate is amazing," Ashton said still absorbing the work. He walked around the ropes taking it in from different angles.

"Tell me about it. This is incredible. Hands down the best thing I have seen all night," she said while brushing her hair behind her right ear, still in awe herself.

"Hands down," he said softly in response while looking at her fondly as he spoke.

"What is time…" she said in almost a whisper and with an upswing at the end of her words turning it into a prompted question.

"I don't know… what is time?" he said to her with a genuine interest in what her response would be.

"It's wild really… I feel like my thoughts on this are being so accurately depicted right in front of my eyes. It's just an illusion, and it really doesn't matter in the grand scheme of things. It's just a way for us to maintain some form of structure and help us all make a bit more sense of our presence and purpose here… I think. I don't know. What do you think? Do I sound like a whack job right now?"

"Will you still like me if I say yes?" he said flatlined.

She gave him a look of surprise and slight disgust at his response.

He broke into a light laugh and said, "I'm kidding. You don't sound like a whack job. Just someone who thinks a lot and is into philosophy." Ashton stood with his hands in his pockets kicking an imaginary rock with his left foot as he stepped forward.

"Time is a unit of measurement to me. I don't have anything too deep for you on this. I am not the modern-day philosopher here, oh great one," he continued.

She didn't like this sarcastic streak and the snark that had begun to creep out.

"Okay... I'm sorry that I asked," she said as she moved to another side of the structure to gain some space from him.

They spent another ten minutes or so pondering time and found their way to the small bar in the back to pick up a glass of complimentary Champagne and found their way to a mini lecture occurring in a side room speaking on Sustainability Through Art. Things had returned to a positive dynamic between them once Ashton tripped leaving the lecture and they were able to share a laugh together.

"You ready to get out of here?" Ashton asked once the tension between them had finally alleviated.

She looked around for Zai, who was nowhere to be found. She was beginning to feel tired and could use a good night's sleep. With Zai still not reappearing after a few minutes of exploring the gallery floor, she took out her phone and sent her a text: *"Heading out with Ashton. You and your art are amazing. See you in the am. Call me naughty and slap my wrist if you see Ashton tomorrow morning."*

She locked her phone, slipped it into the red clutch with the gold clasp and chain she had been carrying for the evening.

"Yep. I'm ready. Let's get out of here. I just need to make a quick stop at the ladies' room on our way out."

"Go ahead. You head on over there and I'll go grab our coats," he said with a charming look in his eyes.

16

They walked the city streets with only a couple of inches between them. She found herself looking around absorbing the city she now called home.

"So, I hope I don't offend you with this question..." Ashton started as he moved a couple inches closer and interlaced his arm with hers.

Oh God... what the hell is this going to be? she thought.

He continued. "Do you by any chance... smoke herb?"

She burst out laughing. "Oh thank God! I had no idea what you were going to say! You really had me nervous for a second. Ashton, I just moved here from Denver. What do you think?"

"Fair. Great. Cool. Okay, well my place isn't too far from here. Any chance you have any interest coming by, sharing a j before we call it a night?"

"You know... I wouldn't mind that at all. I would actually love that," she said with a genuine peaceful demeanor.

"It is either a seven-minute or so subway or a fourteen-minute walk. What do you think?" he asked as he looked down at her boots considering her feet might be getting sore and tired.

"Let's walk," she said confidently. "It's a lovely evening out here."

"Indeed it is, my lady. Indeed it is," he said as they continued to walk with their arms intertwined.

17

Ashton's apartment was reflective of his success in his career. It was a one-bedroomed place with a full bathroom, living area with brick-exposed wall, and a kitchen the perfect size for a single bachelor in Manhattan. His classic gentleman style rang through the apartment, and she noticed two pictures of people she assumed were his family as she walked through the hall and took off her boots.

Ashton had gone right to his bedroom to his night stand where he kept his rolling papers and ganja. He came in and joined her on the couch. As he rolled them a joint, she asked him about the people in the photos. He told her that it was his mother, sister, and cousin who had lived with them growing up in Hoboken. His mother still lived there meanwhile his sister was out in California and no one had known where his cousin ended up for the last three years or so.

The way he rolled his joint was something like she had never seen. There was a distinct style that she has never seen before. He used two papers and connected them with his saliva making an extra-long single paper. He then made a spliff blend with his tobacco and bud. It made for a very large joint. He rolled it effortlessly creating a cone shape.

He pinched the wider end with his thumb and pointer finger and shook it back and forth packing the contents tightly to the bottom. Once the contents were packed tightly, he twisted the wide end a few times and then displayed the most beautiful joint she had ever seen. She couldn't pretend she wasn't impressed and told him that she had just taken extensive notes in her mind.

He lit the joint with the Zippo lighter engraved with the initials, A.L. He took a long inhale with his eyes closed, held in the hit, and then released in with a huge sigh of stress relief. He took two more hits and then passed it along. She took a deep pull herself and allowed it to fill her with the smooth calmness it tended to provide her.

They shared the joint and she tapped out after the fourth time it was handed back to her. He dubbed it out and laid back against the back of the couch with his hands behind his head. She slouched into the couch a bit with her hands on her thighs. They sat in silence for a bit, diving into the depths of their own minds, co-existing in the moment.

"Well this day turned into a very spontaneous enjoyable day," he finally said.

"Yea, this was a really nice day. Thank you for being a part of it, Ashton," she said in return with her head still against the back of the couch but looking in his direction.

Ashton took her by surprise. He peeled himself from the back of the couch and leaned forward and placed his hand on her right thigh. She looked at him with a look of a bit of confusion but also desire. He pounced on her and began to kiss her hard. She kissed him back at first, but with his tongue deep in her mouth she found herself pulling back slightly.

Ashton lifted his head and studied her reaction. He could tell she was torn on what she wanted her next move to be. He began to kiss her again in hopes of turning her on. He kissed on her neck and lightly wrapped his hand around her neck, implying that he can and will if that is what she is into. She let out a slight moan, because she could not pretend that the combination of his soft lips and tongue on her collarbone as he lightly cut off her airway made her wet. As soon as she started to get into it again, her mind started talking her out of the moment once more.

The marijuana had gone to her head. She found herself analyzing everything and unable to stay in the moment. She pulled back once again. Ashton stood up and took off his pants. In what felt like seconds, Ashton was now standing in front of her with no pants, no boxers. He did however decide to keep on his socks and shirt. At this point she didn't know what to say. She had never had a man expose himself before it was clear that she was completely into it (especially like this). *At least have me touch it through your pants at least once before giving the full show.* she thought while processing what was happening. She gave him a look full of shock and nerves.

He grabbed her hands and pulled her upright. He kissed her with his right hand around the back of her head and the left around her lower back. He was a great kisser; she couldn't deny that. Something just didn't feel right though; she couldn't let herself give in to the moment and embrace the sexual healing that Ashton was longing to give her. Maybe it was because in the back of her mind she was thinking about Mike. She hadn't been with anyone since him. It felt like forever ago since she had a casual hookup with someone. She pulled away slightly again, with their foreheads touching and making eye contact with one another.

As Ashton read her reflecting eyes and could tell that she wasn't comfortable; he took a step back and his response blew her away.

"Okay. This is just getting awkward. I'm going to have to ask you to leave."

"What?"

"No, everything is cool. I am just going to have to ask you to leave right now. I don't want to waste any more of your time."

"Are you kicking…"

"Yes. I mean, we are cool. We are good. Welcome to the city, and I had a great time. It was great connecting, but I am going to have to ask you to leave right now."

It took her a minute or two to comprehend what was happening and what he was requesting.

Is he really kicking me out of his apartment right now? Because I don't want to put him inside of me at this very moment?

She started to walk towards her shoes, and he walked over to his pants that were lying on the floor. He nodded at her giving her positive reinforcement to her actions in preparing to go.

"I really don't understand... we have had a great day; I am really just not ready to get naked and fuck you, Ashton."

"No. It's cool. Really. We are totally good. Again, welcome to the city. I'm really glad we got to have the day together. It's all good. Text me. It's all good."

"Text you? Like really text you? Or you just saying that to try to not be the biggest douchebag in West Manhattan?"

Those words bounced off him; she could tell this wasn't the first time that something like this had happened in this apartment.

"Just text me. We are good. Welcome to the city, get home safe, and have a wonderful rest of your night," Ashton said as he gave her a kiss on the cheek and gently guided her out the door with his hand on her left shoulder. Immediately, he closed the door leaving her alone in his hallway. She could hear the sound of the lock on his door being flipped, fully securing the unwelcomed state that he had just made very clear.

Her steps down his narrow hallway back to the city street were a blur. She was still in shock at what had just happened. It took her until she had hit the corner and turned that it really had just hit her.

What a dick. Thank God, I didn't let him put it in me. But God, I kind of wish I had. I would have loved to have an orgasm right now, plus, he was hot. She laughed to herself at the madness of how that series of events had just happened. *Welcome to the city. What an entrance to dating in the city*, she thought as she made her way to her subway stop and headed underground to make her way back to her apartment.

18

"So how was the rest of *your* night?" Zai asked opening the fridge to grab a coconut water.

She looked over her shoulder while making eggs on the stove top, "I can guarantee it is not going to be anything like you are expecting me to say."

"Oh, was it super kinky? Please do tell girl... I love sex stories," Zai said leaning over the counter.

"We never got to sex. He kicked me out before I ever got naked," she said as she put the spatula down on the counter and turned to face Zai. She leaned against the counter with her elbows propped up behind her.

"What do you *mean* he kicked you out? What happened?"

She went into the story of what happened and by the end Zai was still leaning against the counter with her jaw on the floor.

"Girl, I have heard some stories before. This one is up there. I think my favorite part is the fact that he ended up being with his pants off before you were into it. Like, that is kind of creepy... rape-like"

"In his defense, it never felt rape-like, I must admit. But it was definitely weird. Oh, did I mention that he had his pants off, completely naked waist down, but still had on his shirt?"

They both broke into hysterical laughter. She was really grateful to have Zai to share this story with the next morning instead of internalizing and waiting until she and Casey jumped on a call later that week.

"What's so funny ladies?" Benjamin said as he stretched his arms over his head and joined them around the corner close to the dining room table.

"Good morning, handsome. Our new gal pal here just had her first experience with a city douchebag," Zai said, filling Benjamin in. She instinctively shot Zai a look wishing she hadn't shared that with Benjamin, even though she had no reason to not share it with him.

"Ugh, buzzkill. Sorry to hear that. City is full of them. Pretty safe to say it won't be the last one, gotta be honest. Onward and upwards. Now be a gem and toss me a coconut water from the fridge, would you?" Benjamin responded.

She felt so much better about everything after seeing how relatively normal this was, and she was grateful that she didn't put out and give it up to Ashton. She went from disappointed, to embarrassed, to empowered. *Today is going to be a good day.* she thought while looking at her two new friends.

"So listen…" Benjamin interjected to the silence that had fallen amongst them all. "I think the time has come that we all need to sit around a table all together and eat, drink, and be merry."

"You don't have to tell me twice. I have rehearsal tonight, tomorrow night, and every night this week. But maybe next Wednesday night?"

"Next Wednesday works for me," she said after pretending to think about what was coming up on her very empty schedule.

"Next Wednesday it is. Let me know what you guys are in the mood for as it gets closer, and we will make it happen."

Benjamin knocked on the counter twice and made his way back to his bedroom to get dressed for work. She thought, *somebody is a House of Cards fan'* as he walked away. She liked it; she was a huge *House of Cards* fan herself.

Zai shared one of her most recent horror stories from a date before she came over and gave her a kiss on the cheek and made her way to her room herself.

There she was again, the center of her two new roommates and friends who were orbiting around her with their own hustle and bustle to tend to. She was ready to make her mark and create her own hustle in the city. She pushed against the counter, mocked Benjamin to herself with two knocks, and headed to her bedroom to get dressed for the day.

19

*T*he next Wednesday had arrived and she found herself back at her new favorite café, the one that had the picture of the Manhattanhenge that resonated with her deeply the first time she had visited. She had grown comfortable with the workers there and this place had become her go-to spot. The place she felt most comfortable. She was scrolling through LinkedIn and other job posting sites reaching out to recruiters she thought would be a good fit for her and her Consulting experience. It didn't take long to receive a message back from a local recruiter. It read:

"Hi, thank you so much for reaching out in regard to finding employment. I'm with Smith-Johnson recruiting firm here right in Manhattan, New York. After taking a look at your résumé I think we may be able to find a great fit and work well together. I have an availability to speak with and learn more about you at eleven thirty today, does this work with your availability?"

She was ecstatic at how quickly she had heard back and couldn't wait to tell Benjamin and Zai the good news about the opportunities coming her way soon. She opened the group chat that they had just started yesterday morning.

"Believe it or not...a recruiter has already gotten back to me. jumping on the phone this afternoon."

"I believe it and I'm not surprised at all... you are amazing. If you are half as good at working as you are at living, you're a rock star in the professional world," Benjamin replied.

"Hell yeah girlfriend! That's an extra round of drinks tonight at dinner," Zai replied.

"Oh yes, dinner!" Benjamin chimed in. *"How do you guys feel about Indian?"*

She didn't want to tell her true feelings; truth was it gave her heartburn every time, but she didn't want to be that girl. She stopped and realized how ridiculous she was being. She was acting like a teenager. Yet, it still wasn't enough for her to speak up and suggest something else.

"Hell yes, Zai. I never turn down Indian food. I am all in."

Now she really felt awful for saying she didn't want to go. She knew that was silly; they were all grown adults and they wouldn't care.

Despite her dissatisfaction on the decision and her desire to request something else, she watched her fingers type and send: *"I'm in."*

"Great!" Zai chimed in. *"There's a great place over on Pel Street called the Curry House. See you there eight thirty?"*

"Cheers see you there," Benjamin replied.

"Ciao," she wrote.

She dove back into her computer exploring the different job opportunities and began to imagine herself working in these different offices here in Manhattan. It had been what feels like forever since she's been in a professional setting, but she was ready to dive in and make it happen. She didn't want to ever go back to where she was a couple of years ago, and she knew that she didn't want to be a part of someone else's dream like she had been with Mike's hummus collaboration. She was finding great joy in exploring her daydreams imagining herself being a part of a new team and constructing a new chapter that activates what feels like an entire new life.

That afternoon she jumped on a call with the recruiter from the Smith-Johnson recruiting agency. Gabrielle had a very assertive demeanor. Made her feel comfortable that she was in good hands for landing an opportunity. Their conversation was rather brief; Gabrielle wanted to know her background and what she was looking for in her next opportunity, as she worked on finding what it was she was looking for, here in the city. Gabrielle sounded confident that they'd be able to find an opportunity for her amongst one of the postings they currently had. She couldn't help but be skeptical that that is something Gabrielle said to every person that she speaks with. They ended the call with scheduling a face-to-face interview for Friday afternoon for the next formal step in the recruitment process.

When they got off the phone, she found herself following the train of her thoughts. From her daydreams earlier while exploring jobs to then speaking with the recruiter, it was almost hard to believe how quickly things were coming to fruition as she was just enjoying her time in the city. Everything has felt like magic since arriving to NYC. By simply having fun and keeping optimistic that is all going to work out... things have been.

What is it that I really did want to do? I haven't had a real plan before or since coming here. What kind of company do I see myself with?

She could feel the wheels in her mind beginning to speed up. Simultaneously, her heart began to race creating discomfort in her body. Before anxious thoughts could take control once again, she took a sip of her peppermint tea with her eyes closed.

As always, she reflected on conversations that she had with Casey in the past about staying in the moment and enjoying the journey. She smiled as she could hear Casey's voice and saw her face as she focused on it: "I always turn to yoga and my breath when I start to feel overwhelmed or start doubting myself and my journey..."

She took a deep inhale through her nose and exhaled through her mouth.

"Maybe I should go take a yoga class today," she said herself. *"Anytime I went with Casey in Denver, it did help."*

She pulled out her phone and downloaded the app ClassPass. *3:30 p.m.: Kundalini Yoga*. She had never done Kundalini and she wasn't even exactly sure what it was. She overheard some yogis in Trader Joe's once having a love session over it, but beyond that, that was all she had. She redirected her focus to Google to find more.

Popping up on the screen she scrolled to find the first things that the internet had to say: *"Kundalini yoga is a form of yoga that involves chanting, singing, breathing exercises, and repetitive poses. Its purpose is to activate your Kundalini energy, or shakti. This is a spiritual energy that's said to be located at the base of your spine."*

She looked at her screen, a bit intimidated. After a couple of deep breaths and movements… she shrugged and said to herself, *"Fuck it. Everything else here is new, you might as well try this too. Am I ready for kundalini energy? Well, I'm not really sure, I don't know what it will be like…"*

She slipped her phone into her pocket and headed back to the apartment to get changed and head over to the studio.

20

With her go-to yoga outfit, she scrambled through her belongings looking for her mat she could have sworn she packed from Colorado.

"Where is it? I could have sworn I packed it!" she said under her breath as she tossed various belongings from one side of the room to the other. With a final puff of breath she threw her hands up and decided to go on without it; she didn't know exactly where the studio was and didn't want to be late.

Making her way towards the subway she noticed a sensation of nervousness moving through her system. *What is this about? I've never been nervous about going to a yoga class before*, she thought as she pulled out her MetroCard walking down the Washington Square Park Subway stop. The playlist that Zai shared with her the other day began to flood through her headphones. With the first few notes a sense of peace and gratitude filled her body. There was something so magical about Zai – everything she does adds a touch of beauty, grace, and upliftment to the moment.

As the subway slowed down and the words 'Essex St Delancy' appeared on the wall. She shifted herself out of her seat and stepped in front of the doors so that as soon as they opened, she could make her way out to find sunlight and fresh air once again. Navigating the street traffic, making note of a few more restaurants and shops that seem worthy of trying sooner than later. She turned right onto Stanton, and as she walked up, she had an illuminated white neon light displaying 'Victory'. In the window she saw a boutique store in the front, and then her eyes settled onto the largest gong she had ever seen in the back of the studio. As she looked through the glass at the other people already in the studio, she noticed they were all wearing all white. As a large knot formed in her throat, she scanned her outfit and started judging herself as she had on her favorite all-black yoga outfit.

A minor panic took over her and as she almost fled from class, another woman wearing a white tank top, white yoga pants, white turban, and a colorful shawl walked past her and noticed the inner turmoil she was exuding.

"You're welcome any way and at any time in these classes… come on in. *Sat Nam*," she said and walked in holding the door open making it near impossible to back out now.

Walking in and scanning the floor, she slipped off her shoes and had them join the collection of shoes on the floor that varied in style. Seeing a range of shoes from Crocs to Gucci slip-ons she felt a level of comfort and trusting that this is one of those studios that truly doesn't judge. Looking around still feeling awkward that she was the only one in the building that wasn't wearing all white, she walked around the small storefront breathing in the array of crystals, books, and facial oils towards the wall of various white clothing items hanging.

"I really don't think this is my style," she said to herself pulling out the long flowing white dresses.

"You really don't have to wear white in class if you don't want to," the yogi behind the counter said in a very grounded and centered demeanor as if being able to read her thoughts.

"Yea? It seems like we do," she replied immediately making a face that screamed *I spoke too quickly* and hoped she didn't offend.

The woman behind the counter laughed. "You're going to get along with this community just fine. We like humor and sarcasm around here. It's a part of the lineage best practices to wear white—but nothing is ever a requirement."

"I like that… lessens the feels of a cult. What is the deal with the white clothes then?"

"We get 'it's a cult' thing all the time. It's pretty interesting to look at that. I'll answer you about the white clothes thing in a moment too—even if it were a cult, which it isn't!" she said really sharply to get that point across. "We practice a yoga technology that allows for the optimization of mind, body, and spirit. These practices literally help you become more aligned with your best self and release layers of fear, falsity, and self-doubt. And we celebrate everyone being fully their own unique expression of their truth. Would be a pretty great cult to join if you were to ask me."

She really appreciated this woman's essence and demeanor. She felt so comfortable and simultaneously uplifted and activated by being in the space and making eye contact with her.

"Yea okay, I'm in. So I'd like to take the next class coming up... do I sign up with you here?"

"Yes, you can fill out this form and then I'll get you into the system," the woman said while handing her a clipboard.

"Oh! And the white clothes?" she said with a strong curiosity.

"Ah yes, so every color carries a different frequency which then impacts our auric expression and how other energies can work with us. Yogi Bhajan who brought the Kundalini practice over to the West from the Sikh tradition taught and is continued to be taught that the auric field of an individual extends out about six feet. When we wear white, it adds about another foot onto us helping to amplify our frequency, adding more protection to us from negative energies, and makes us more magnetic for prosperity and abundance," she replied.

"Oh... wow. That's deep."

"Yea, everything we do here is pretty deep and expansive. The layers keep going," she said with a soft laugh under her voice.

Nodding and taking this information in, she found herself putting down the clipboard and walking back over to the wall of the white clothing. She ran her hands through the rack and settled on a white jumper that seemed to be a high-quality piece. The first time she looked through the rack she didn't let herself pick it up because she browsed the price tag and said she wasn't spending that type of money today. She was now holding it and falling in love with it as she held it up to herself looking in the mirror.

"You really don't have to wear white, especially for your first class. But I have to admit, that looks really cute on you, and this is before you are even really wearing it," she said looking back at her with softer eyes and a true level of care.

"Right!? I'm really in love with it. I told myself I wasn't going to spend money today, so I am trying to practice self control."

"I fully support your decision either way. My teacher from this lineage always use to say a few different things about shopping. One, it fuels the soul - buy the thing. And also, when there is something that costs more than you are comfortable spending, give yourself permission to elevate yourself into the person that would be able to afford that with no problem. Timeline hop. Today in class they will be doing a prosperity meditation, so who knows... you may manifest that $180 by the end of class. Again, I'm really not trying to make you do anything!" she said sincerely.

The level of wisdom, information, and ease this woman was able to share with her was highly impressive. She was curious who this teacher of hers was. Through that brief conversation she felt so empowered and motivated to be the boss babe she knew she was at her core.

"I'm getting this, please and thank you. Can you charge the class and those to this card?"

"Yes. The class is going to begin shortly. Do you want to leave the card with me, and I'll take care of it while you're in class and you can get it when you are done?"

"That would be perfect. Thank you so much! And your name again?"

"Charan Teja Kaur."

"A pleasure to meet you," she slowly began to try to say her name back, "Chara..." and found herself pause and forget the rest

"Charan Teja Kaur," she told her again with a soft laugh. "The bathroom is all the way in the back. Turn at the steps next to the stage and you'll see two on the side before the outdoor patio."

"You have an outdoor patio?" she said excited.

"Yes. Feel free to peek, but class is going to begin so maybe take a look after class is finished."

"Sounds good. Thank you again."

"Sat Nam". Charan Teja Kaur said as she turned around to immerse herself back into the computer.

Why does everyone keep saying that? Sat Nam? What does that mean?" she thought as she made her way into the back of the studio. Turning her head side to side breathing in the Buddhist art work covering the walls and dancing around yogis in all white that have set themselves up for class already.

After putting on the all-white overalls, she took a look at herself in the tall mirror hanging on the door and a huge smile came over her face. She was radiant! 'Wow, I'm in love!" She came out of the bathroom feeling light and excited. Finding a spot towards the back of the room, she placed her items to the side, grabbed a yoga mat from the extras she spotted on the wall, and sat down settling into the space. She felt amazing. There was something about this space that was effortlessly making her feel lighter, brighter, and expanded. *"This was a great life decision today."* As she took a few deep breaths, the teacher stepped up onto the stage, sitting on what appeared to be some kind of animal skin blanket in front the massive gong. Adjusting the mic, she shifted in her seat, took a deep breath and said, "*Sat Nam* everyone, let us begin to rub our hands together to tune in."

Rocking side to side in her seat a bit finding a center, she looked around at everyone else to get clarity of what she was supposed to be doing. She brought her palms together at the center of her chest and began to rub them together vigorously. She felt charged already.

"Begin slowing down the movement of the hands allowing your hands to find a sense of stillness pressed together at the center of the chest. Thumbs meeting the sternum, elongating the spine finding an extra half of inch in the spine. Deep inhale to tune in." Everyone took a deep inhale through their nose and held it. "And exhale," the teacher said as people deeply exhaled. "And inhale to tune in," the teacher said once again. She took a deep inhale feeling confident and then what happened next left her unsure and a bit insecure.

"*Onggggggggg Namoooooo Guru Devvvvvvv Namoooooooo.*

Onggggggg   Namoooooo   Guru   Devvvvvvv Namoooooooo.

Onggggggg   Namoooooo   Guru   Devvvvvvv Namoooooooo."

The class recited this very loudly in unison. She just sat there feeling the sounds in a way that she had never experienced sound before. This was not like any yoga class she had ever been to, and they were literally just starting. The group continued after a long inhale, where instructed to press the palms together, squeeze the energy up the spine, press their tongue to the roof of the mouth, and focus at the third eye center. There was another round of chants said that she had no idea what was said. Finding herself wanting to judge herself and was becoming unpresent she made the decision to surrender fully to what was happening and just go with it.

The class continued and it was the strangest experience! Unlike the other yoga classes she had been to where it was a fluid series of posture and breath. There was a more step by step procedure for different intentions the teacher had chosen to focus on. They began with a CatCow posture. Even that was different! Rather than fluid and gentle and connecting with the breath. There were instructions to move a steady pace, and on the inhale, say in their minds *"sat"* and on the exhale *"nam"*. She found herself slightly annoyed with how much this phrase was being said, without having any idea what is was. *Is this really a cult? Am I being brainwashed?* she thought as she found herself in child's pose opening her eyes looking down at her body now wearing the white jumper.

After an hour and a half of different postures, breathwork, poses, and lying still to the gong being played, she heard an angelic song fill the space and the teachers voice coming back over the sound system, "begin to wiggle the fingers and the toes… rolling the ankles and the wrists… bring the soles of the feet and the palms of the hands together rubbing them together… turn side to side getting in a nice cat stretch…"

As she followed the guidance of the teacher and she returned to her body, she was in awe of how amazing she felt. She was so light, energized, and clear. "Bringing the knees into the chest, roll up and down the spine a few times making your way back to seated to close class." Feeling like a child again, she rolled up and down on her spine springing back up to a seat posture on the final roll, she settled in with a smile on her face.

"Bringing palms together at the heart space, breathing in to close." Learning from how they started class she decided to breathe and simply observe how this group of unique and next level yogis close a class.

The teacher opened her mouth and began to sing in an angelic voice, "May the long-time sun shine upon you. All love surround you. And the pure light within you, guide your way on. Guide your way on. Guide your way on." She took a deep inhale and then followed with, *"Saaaaaaaat Nam. Saaaaaaaat Nam. Saaaaaaat Nam. Sat Nam* everyone, thank you for your practice. Have a beautiful day." She bowed her head to the floor, and everyone did the same.

Following suit, she brought her forehead to the ground while thinking to herself *What the fuck is sat nam!?*

Putting away her yoga mat and integrating the shifts she was feeling, she found herself doing a little shimmy shake and dance. She felt amazing! Slightly embarrassed that she had just done that, she looked around to see if anyone noticed. They didn't. The class immediately started to turn to other classmates who they had clearly known and practiced with for a bit. A sense of wanting this camaraderie with these people began to grow in her. She scanned the art work a bit more and looked down at her body to make sure that it was still her. She felt so different—in a good way. As she made her way up to the front of the studio again, she met eyes with Charan Teja Kaur. She didn't need to say much for how she was feeling to be understood.

"I know, right? Charan Teja Kaur said. "Welcome. My life changed dramatically when I started practicing Kundalini. Hope you'll be coming back."

"Yea, I definitely think I'll be coming back again. I live pretty close by too so it's not hard to get here."

"Oh great. Nothing is too hard to get to in the city if the desire to be there is strong enough anyway—I totally get it."

Who is this woman? She drops so much wisdom effortlessly every time she speaks, she thought.

"Yes, for sure. By the way... what does *'sat nam'* mean? I've heard it so many times and was even saying it and I have no idea what I'm saying."

"*Sat Nam*. Truth is my identity. *'Sat'* means truth. *'Nam'* means name or identity. So when you bring it together, *'Sat Nam'*, we are saying to ourselves and mirroring back to others that truth is my identity. Truth is your identity."

She stared back at her a bit dumbfounded and taken aback of how profound this was. She took a gulp of air. "Wow," she finally said. *"Sat Nam."*

"I know, many layers and really deep this technology is, I told you. Oh by the way, here is your card. You're all set. Sat Nam."

"Oh thank you! I totally forgot! See you soon."

"Thanks for coming, have a great day," Charan Teja Kaur said, unphased by the shifts of energy that were being experienced in her body as she settled into this new teaching.

Stepping back out into the streets with her bag over her shoulder that now held her black yoga outfit. she was seeing everything around her a bit brighter. She noticed a lightness in her walk and a soft smile on her face...

I'm still not exactly sure what I just experienced, but holy fuck I love how I feel right now, she thought as she put her headphones on and put on her favorite playlist to jam to. She scooped up a fresh green juice and made her way back to the apartment to relax and integrate all that had happened in those last couple of hours before getting ready for dinner with Zai and Benjamin.

21

*A*t 8.40 p.m. she walked into the Curry House and scoped the restaurant to see if she was the first to arrive or if either Zai or Benjamin had beat her there. The restaurant was really cute. Indian royalty came to her mind when she walked in. *Such as most restaurants in the city, no?* It was on the small side with about sixteen to twenty tables if she had to guess. They were lucky to be seated right away and they gathered around their small table towards the middle of the restaurant. She made sure to shuffle herself around to get the chair that faced where she could see the door.

Zai raised her hand and waved her over; she was wearing a pale orange dress that looked incredible against her complexion. She was blown away by Zai's natural beauty every time she saw her still. Zai carries a strong silent confidence to her that makes her even more attractive beyond the beautiful face and body she has been blessed with.

"Benjamin texted me a couple of minutes ago. He is running late. He told me to order drinks and get him a glass of wine," Zai said as she joined her at the table.

"Cool. Sounds good. What are you drinking tonight?"

"Something strong. This director is killing me. I'm telling you, I will never work for this company again after this production. There hasn't been a single rehearsal that has gone smoothly in his eye. I mean, I'm an artist—I get it! He wants it to be perfect. But let me tell you… I don't like to toot my own horn but goddammit, toot-toot! We are killing this production!" She let out a frustrated sigh and softly pulled on the ends of her afro.

She didn't know what the right thing to say was. She had never been in a production. She had danced for a brief period of her life, but there was no director of that show. And she wasn't exactly ready to share that fun fact about herself… if she was ever going to, that is.

"I'm sorry girlfriend. It'll be show time before you know it. Just keep showing up and shining bright like I am sure you are."

"Aw that was really sweet! Thank you!" she smiled, and she could tell that she had chosen her words well because she helped to release some of the tension Zai was holding just a few moments ago. "You look extra radiant right now… how was your day? Did you get laid or something?"

She laughed, "No! I actually went to a kundalini yoga class… it was the most bizarre experience I have ever had perhaps ever. Definitely within all of my yoga experiences for sure… but I feel amazing! Like, radiant is a great word for it. I feel radiant. Have you ever done it?"

"Never even heard of it. Good for you though girl. Looks good on you. Can we pick our drinks, please?

Benjamin wants us to order him a glass of red." Zai said back with a shortness in her tonality. It was beyond obvious that she was at a breaking point of frustration with the production she was working.

"You know... I'm not feeling like drinking tonight after that class. I might get a mocktail, but regardless, yes let's get you a drink girl," she said scanning the restaurant for someone to flag down to order.

She looked through the menu suddenly feeling a slight pressure to make a decision for Benjamin. She ran her finger down the list, slowly reading all the options under the California wines until she came across the 2006 Holdrege Russian River Valley Pinot Noir. She had this wine for the first time with one of teh first meals she ever had in Denver. She loved the richness that danced on her palate that night and every night since.

She ordered a mojito mocktail, and Zai decided to go with an Indian beer on the menu. By the time the drinks had arrived, Benjamin was meeting them at the table.

"And how are my two favorite ladies on the Lower East Side doing this evening?" he asked as he took off his coat and hung it on the back of his chair.

"Better now that you are here," she said in an innocent and playful way.

"Oh, I like that! You keep that tone up young lady!" he said returning her playfulness.

"I'm starving guys. Can we make some quick executive decisions on what we are eating?" Zai said clearly feeling the frustration that had been released moments ago returning to her once again.

"I get the same thing every time. I'm good," Benjamin said putting his hands up to stay out of the line of fire of Zai's hangriness. He held his wine glass by the stem, swirled the contents of his glass, held it up to his lips with his nostrils in the glass (it was clear he had taken wine-tasting classes at some point in his life) and then took a sip allowing the first taste to be savored on his tongue.

"Wow. This is delicious. Fantastic choice," Benjamin said loudly, extending the glass to her to try.

"I have. Had it back in Denver years ago and it is my go-to. I was really happy to see it on their menu. I'm glad you like it too. It's nerve-racking calling the big shots like this!" she said holding her glass us to cheers her two roommates.

"Speaking of making decisions, I don't go out and eat Indian too often, so I could use some guidance on what I should go for here."

"I never understand how people don't go out for Indian all the time," Zai said to Benjamin looking for reassurance which was surprisingly provided with a nod from Benjamin the moment she started speaking.

"Do you like spicy? And when I say spicy… I mean spicy!" Benjamin looked her in the eyes and did a playful bite in the air. They all laughed.

"Speaking spicy… I am just going to call the kettle black here. You two are being very spicy tonight, I'm just saying. Like… don't go falling in love or anything, okay?"

Everyone at the table (including Zai herself) was taken back from the comment., She didn't premeditate that, and now things had grown a bit awkward at the table.

Zai took a couple sips of her drink, and then finally found some words to formulate. "So, I wasn't trying to make... I just thought we have gotten comfortable... did I make things awkward? I'm sorry."

"You really didn't!" Benjamin said regretting what had just happened. Zai sighed and said, "I don't even know where that just came from. I'm sorry guys, it has just been a really long day and this production... and director... it is all wearing on me something serious. And I am fucking hungry! Let me put in an appetizer before I end up making us all break a lease or something by the end of this meal, goddamn. Never let this girl go eleven hours without eating ever again! Do you guys want anything for an appetizer? I'm going to go hunt down this server with his Indian ass self. He better know next time I need to eat."

"Yes, I do actually," Benjamin said after sitting very still and upright for the last couple of minutes, not wanting to make any sudden moves or actions that might set something off again. "Samosas please. Do you want anything?" he asked turning his eyes in her direction.

She felt she needed to pick something so that they would all have food to be able to focus their attention on sooner than later.

She looked down at the menu and picked the first thing she saw. "Chana puri please."

Zai gave them both a single nod and slid out of her seat in a rushed and urgent way that let them know she was embarrassed of the small scene she had just introduced to the group.

The remaining two sat staring down at the table for a couple of seconds unsure of what the next thing to do was.

"So, that was awkward. I didn't think we were doing anything…"

"Yea, no. I didn't think we were doing anything other than just being friendly and fun…" she replied not needing him to finish his sentence.

"You good?" he said with a weariness to his voice. He was walking on eggshells.

"I'm good. I'm a little hungry—but don't worry, I don't get anywhere near the hangriness that Zai apparently experiences," she said shifting her eyes around to create another awkward silence but hoping to create a level of humor.

Benjamin took the bait and he let out a well welcomed laugh across the table. They lifted their glasses, clinked finding direct eye contact with one another (the proper way that two people are to make cheers to one another) and took a long sip of their drinks. Zai walked back to the table and before she could say anything, they both held up a hand to stop letting her know that the moment had passed, and everything was fine.

"Let's drink and be merry until the food comes and add that to the to-do list, yes?" Benjamin said with his head titled. Zai nodded and lifted her glass. The other two followed her lead and saluted once more.

Very soon after, the appetizers arrived at the table.

Her chana puri was placed in front of her, and she had no idea what to do with it. She studied the bowl of chickpeas and what looked like to her potatoes and the six fluffy shells that accompanied it, and she cursed herself for picking something off the menu that she had no idea how to eat. She was spared a few minutes of embarrassment by the server asking them for the dinner orders.

"I'll take the Chicken tikka masala," Benjamin said handing his menu to the waiter.

"Chicken? I thought you were vegan" she quickly said after Benjamin made his order.

"What? No! Why did you think I was vegan?" he responded amused.

Everyone including the waiter turned towards her curious of her response. "You were wearing a T-shirt about Clark Kent being a vegan the day you met me..."

"Oh that? I just like it and thought it was funny. I've been vegan before, but my body needs meat these days".

She took a deep breath and was curious why it upset her to feel as if she'd been lied to. She wasn't vegan, what does it matter to her? "Hm, well, okay... assumptions. All they do is make an ass out of you and me, right?"

"Aw, don't make a thing out of it" Benjamin said feeling her getting sensitive, "and right" he said playfully nudging her with his elbow.

"Well, now that that is cleared up, make that two chicken tikka masalas please," Zai added.

"Well, third is a charm, right?" she said and turned her head slightly feeling that was such an awkward way to say that.

"Three chicken tikka masalas. Got it. Thank you very much," the server said, giving Zai a look of slight fear. She had really shaken him up. She couldn't blame him though. She probably would be a little fearful of someone that had cornered them in the back of a restaurant demanding they had food put in. Poor Zai, she was just a hungry overworked artist. The struggle... it can be real.

The tension amongst the three of them subsided. Zai taught her how to properly eat her chana puri, creating a hole in the shell and stuffing it with the other components on her dish, and they all continued to drink. Zai ordered a second beer, while Benjamin made the decision to order a bottle of wine.

Over dinner, they discussed her conversation with the recruiter earlier that day, a couple of the hundred different ways Zai has come up with to murder her director, and the latest project Benjamin has been working on in the lab: a simulator to help in chiropractor adjustments. They were three very different people who had a healthy and intriguing synergy amongst them—much like the culture of New York City at large.

By the time the check had come, they all had full bellies and a strong buzz. She was amazed how she felt tipsy, as if she had been drinking, but she didn't have a sip of alcohol the whole meal. Benjamin pulled out his card and insisted that this meal be on him. They put up an argument and offered to Venmo him as they pulled out their phones. He refused and made them promise that they would both take him out for a meal by themselves and pay for it instead. They smiled and agreed thinking it was a fair and enjoyable trade-off.

22

*T*he three of them walked into their building together and were greeted by Ron's pleasant smile.

"Well, well, well, if it isn't the two most beautiful girls in New York City. And then you have this guy that you drag along with you," Ron said playfully putting his hand out to shake Benjamin's hand.

"Oh c'mon now Ron, act like we don't have the bromance of all time brewing here. I know you think about me during the day. And you know I daydream about having biceps like these someday, you gotta tell me your secret some time." Benjamin played back with him shaking his hand and grabbing Ron's bicep with the other hand. They both laughed and the girls looked at each other smiling shaking their heads.

"Well done with the new addition, guys. She is a keeper. The last roommate, she was nice but… I don't know…"

"We agree," Zai and Benjamin said in unison. The three of them laughed. She just smiled enjoying the buzzing energy moving through her. The three roommates said their farewells to Ron and began their trek up the four flights of stairs.

When they got back to the apartment Zai threw her leftovers in the fridge and gave them both a kiss on the cheek and thanked them for a lovely evening all together and headed off to bed. She had double rehearsal tomorrow, and she was taking advantage of every moment of rest and sleep that she could get when she could get them. The remaining two headed into their bedrooms and slipped into sweats and T-shirts, returning to the living area once they were both more comfortable.

She claimed the papasan, sitting with her legs crossed and her hands behind her head rested up against the top half of the chair. Benjamin took a seat on the floor with his back against the sofa being sandwiched with the kidney shaped coffee table in front of him. They shared an enjoyable silence for a bit.

"I have a question for you," Benjamin finally said.

"Mmm...?" she replied, not having much of a desire to say too much and also a bit nervous of where this was going after the slight shenanigans that occurred around the dinner table this evening.

"Do you smoke herb?" he said bluntly.

She opened her eyes and smiled, pleasantly surprised at the question that came out. "I do. Why? Do you?"

"I do. And I really want to smoke a bowl right now. You in?"

"I've had an amazing day, full belly, and from Denver... of course I am in!" she said leaning over herself putting her fist out to Benjamin to offer a fist-bump.

Benjamin smiled and returned the pound with an explosion of his hand once their knuckles touched, stood up from his seated position without any hands, and went back to his room returning with a metal tin he held with both hands in front of himself. She extended her spine to see what was on the tin as he returned to his seated position on the floor placing the tin on the table.

"A Mighty Mouse lunch box, eh?" she said highly amused at her findings.

"Damn skippy, a Mighty Mouse lunch box! I have had this lunch box since I was in the 4th grade. My mom held on to it for a bunch of years, and then three years or so ago when she and I got together, she brought it for me. She had been cleaning out the garage and she found a box of a bunch of my old stuff. She would be so proud to know her anti-religious son is now using the lunch box she used to pack my lunch in for the materials I now use to pack my bowls with," he said and then looked up at her with a close-lipped grin.

"I love it," she said returning the smile except with her teeth exposed and leaned back into her chair enjoying the comfortable silence that the two of them were able to share.

Benjamin packed his grinder and began to twist the top back and forth while staring off into one of Zai's paintings on the wall across from him next to the TV. It was a naked woman who was wrapped in a silk multi-colored cloth, entangled in it, as if she was a trapeze artist winding down from her latest act. She couldn't help but be amused by how small the grinder looked in his massive hands. She hadn't noticed how large Benjamin was. Not bulky, just… big.

Benjamin removed the lid to the grinder, and his large hands delicately removed a large pinch of the pot and placed it in the bowl he had also removed from the Mighty Mouse lunch box. It was black with swirls of orange and red across the surface. Once the emptiness of the bowl had been replaced with the light green ganja, he handed the packed bowl to her, reaching as far as he could knowing she would meet him halfway.

"Ladies first," he said.

"Oh, you shouldn't have… just kidding. You totally should have. Much appreciated, my dear."

"My utmost pleasure, my lady," he said back in an awful pretend English accent. He handed her a lighter as well.

She raised the flame to the bowl touching on just the corner of the pot, being sure to light it respectfully and efficiently. She took a deep inhale allowing the smoke to fill her lungs and the THC to enter her bloodstream. She released her inhale with a deep exhale with eyes closed and a soft content smile on her face. "Ah, now that is lovely," she said has she touched her stomach to her thighs passing the bowl and lighter back to Benjamin with one hand.

"New York's finest right here," he said meeting her halfway for the exchange. "It's delivery service too. You can't beat it. The American dream."

She smiled with her eyes closed letting her buzz and full belly consume her. They passed the bowl back and forth a couple more times, letting there be more silence than conversation between them. She was feeling great and then all of a sudden, she wasn't. She felt a slight rise of acid from her chest... *Great! Heartburn. I knew this was coming,* she thought.

She opened her eyes feeling slightly panicked. This wasn't just heartburn. She felt like she was going to be sick. With a couple of really deep breaths, she felt the feeling subside. She let out a breath of release; must have just been the combination of food, mocktails, and marijuana.

"You okay over there?" Benjamin said observing her actions from the couch. He had moved to lying across the couch.

"Yea... I'm good." She said and then with a short pause followed up with, "I think."

Next thing she knew, she was far from okay. The feeling of nausea coursed through her again and she knew this wasn't a false alarm; the last sensation wasn't a fluke: it was a warning. She quickly got up and rushed to the bathroom knowing that she didn't have long before her stomach released all of its contents. She flung open the door, dropped to her knees, stuck her head in the toilet just in the nick of time. She felt all her strength dissipate right along with the food she had consumed at dinner.

She slumped over the toilet, feeling like what she imagined death to feel like. Benjamin was sitting up on the couch leaning over the back staring toward the bathroom where he could see her hunched over. "Yikes... I know you aren't okay-okay, but are you *okay* sweet pea?" he asked gently.

"Mmm," she responded, nervous if she opened her mouth too much another round of vomit would come to fruition.

She didn't need to open her mouth again to manifest that fear. She felt her body convulse again and she dove her head back deep into the porcelain bowl. When Benjamin heard her vomit again, he got up from the couch and walked into the bathroom to give her some moral support. He sat next to her and rubbed her back.

"Ugh, Benjamin. You don't need to be in here. This is gross, I appreciate it, but I'm fine," she said with her left cheek resting again on the bowl. He reached over and flushed the toilet to remove the awful sight and smell they were now both sharing.

"Lady, I know I don't need to be in here. I made the choice. It's fine. Puking sucks… I got you. I don't have anywhere else to be right now, and this bowl has my head buzzing. I'm sorry that it just rocked your world in the worst way possible."

"Mmm… it's fine. I don't think it was the pot. I don't do well with Indian food usually. Plus the syrup of the mojito, and then just smoking on top… it's all fine. I think it is out of my system. I'll wake up good as new," she said with the words coming out softly and slightly unclear from her lack of energy and cheek being pressed up against the toilet bowl.

"All right young lady, well if you think the storm has passed… let's get your ass to bed. First, please do yourself a favor and brush your teeth," Benjamin said as he stood up from the tiled bathroom floor putting his hands under her arms to help her prop herself up and head to the sink. He held on to her, so she knew that she was supported just in case she felt unbearably weak.

She brushed her teeth with her right hand holding herself up on the sink with her left, looking down at the drain not wanting to look at herself in the mirror knowing that she wasn't going to be happy with the state she was in. She put her toothbrush away, rinsed her mouth with a dixie cup of water, spit it out, and splashed her face with cool water. She rested both hands against the sink and took a deep breath still looking down at the drain.

"I'm carrying you to bed," Benjamin said standing behind her looking at her through the mirror.

"Get out of here Benjamin."

"I'm serious! Come on, let me. I know I can lift you… you are weak, and I couldn't tell you the last time I got to do this for someone. Come on, you are doing *me* the favor. Let me feel like a hero for the night."

She sighed and said, "Okay, fine." She lifted her hands over her head. "Carry me to bed, Benjamin."

He gave a huge smile, and put her right arm around his neck, then bent down and scooped her up from behind the knees cradling her in his arms. He guided them out of the bathroom sideways and watched his every step carefully to make sure that he accomplished this perfectly. He pushed open her bedroom door with his elbow. He was grateful she hadn't closed it all the way making his seamless execution much easier. He slid into the bedroom and headed over to her bed, gently placing her down on the fluffy comforter, folding down the other side to properly tuck her in. He helped her get under the covers. She was turned on her side, and had her eyes closed a couple of breaths away from a deep sleep it seemed.

"Thanks Benjamin," she said half awake.

He put her hair behind her ear and gave her a kiss on the forehead.

"It was my pleasure, beautiful. Goodnight and sweet dreams," he said trying to not let out too much emotion in his 'goodnight'.

He got up and began to walk out. He stopped in her doorway and looked back at her. She was the most beautiful woman he had ever laid eyes on. He sighed and softly closed the door.

Making his way back to the couch, he plopped down, and took another large hit from the bowl and then leaned back against the couch staring back up into the weaves of the naked trapeze artist. Benjamin hadn't felt anything for a woman in a while. And he was hoping that these feelings that stirred up this morning would pass as quickly as her stomach bug.

*T*hree *M*onths *L*ater...

23

"*W*hat do you consider love to be?" she asked as she rolled onto her side placing her head in the palm of her hand, propped up on her elbow. Her soft blonde hair swooped across the left side of her face with the slight breeze blowing the natural waves of her hair out of her face just enough for her to not have to move.

"That is an impossible question. There is no scientific definition for love. But what we do know is that the process of falling in love is a bunch of neurochemical processes mixed in with a bunch of externals occurring in just the right sequence or something for two people to undergo the process we call, falling in love. Something about the person makes their body react towards them in a way no one else can, that causes the body to produce more dopamine. They don't know why it happens really, we just know when two people are in love they produce more of it and makes them feel like a million bucks. Apparently. So *they*, (Benjamin formed air quotes as he spoke) say," he answered without ever losing his eye contact with the branches above him. "Dopamine is the natural feel-good drug. It's in the same family as the other all natural feel-good drugs we know and love." He took another a few quick hits from the joint, breathed in deeply with his eyes closed. With his chin towards the sky, he held in his hit for as long as he could, exhaled, and without turning his head or even opening his eyes, he extended his arm to his side and passed the joint to her.

She knew technically he was right. He was always right… *technically*. She stared down at the shades of blue-and-yellow weaving and overlapping one another in their checkered patterned blanket they shared, in the shade of the tree they decided to spend time under in Central Park. She took a long drag, closed her eyes, and basked in her hit. She slowly opened her eyes, and said in a matter-of-fact tone,

"I know *technically speaking* that these kinds of things make up love and describe what it is. But I want to know what *your* opinion is, Benjamin. What do *you* feel it is? Why do *you* feel it happens? Love is merely a series of emotions. Is it something that we just create? Do you think it is all in our head? How does one person steal your heart forever? Effortlessly? What is happening and why does it happen?"

The words came out so quickly and passionately. It was as though with every word, every sentence, the intensity in her thoughts and speech became greater. He could tell they were not premeditated at all; she was rattling from the heart off the tongue. She was always spitting off so many questions with such urgency for the answers as of late. She took one last deep inhale of her Sour Diesel and put out the perfectly rolled joint which she had finally perfected to an art.

"Why must you question everything?" he replied ever so calmly with his hands behind his head lying back admiring the clouds while enjoying the cool breeze. "By the way... great joint. I always remember you are from Colorado more than any other time when you roll a joint for us."

She hadn't thought about Ashton after that awkward night they shared again up until that moment. He was the one that had taught her how to roll a joint like that. When she watched him that one night in his apartment, she made him walk her through it, before the whole taking off the pants and kicking her out thing.

"Why thank you, sir. I'm from Tennessee originally, but I understand what you mean and I receive the compliment. And why do I question everything? Because I am wise. Why do you accept everything you have ever been told by an authority or read to be the truth? History was written by people with biases and egos too, you know."

Benjamin raised an eyebrow, encouraging her to continue.

"Who are the authors of these books? What makes them know more than I? Everything. *Everything!* Everything in life is nothing more than concepts, theories, and materials. People set their biases to things they learn and are so confident in their mind that they are correct, that they feel they must pass on their ideologies to everyone else. Maybe they're right. And there are a lot of people's ideas and opinions I agree with, but I still question everything. Ya know? If you go by every day not asking a single question and accepting everything, what kind of thinking are you doing? And if you aren't thinking… how much can you really know?"

She took a deep breath and paused. She looked up from one of the six-inch-square shades of blue that she had been looking through the entire time she spoke. Benjamin was looking right at her still from his back, but with his eyes locked and ready to make eye contact at any time she decided to remove her lock with the blues. He smirked at her; his smirk made her feel comfortable instantly every time it crossed his face. She continued her rant, only this time as she spoke, she looked him directly in the eyes.

"Benjamin, you must question everything. Everything. Make up your own answers of what life and love is. It's your life, and if you don't form your own opinion… you'll never really know what life is. What love is. What anything is! Life is custom made for every person, but you have to keep going back and trying it on. Ya know, seeing the different styles on to see what fits you best. I know you know this, or at least you knew this, experimenting in college and what not but…." She quickly looked away as soon as she finished her series of thoughts. She was now wearing a smirk of embarrassment with a pair of reddened cheeks to match.

Benjamin sat letting his wheels turn for a while. Finally, he responded.

"That last part with the suit or whatever and trying on clothes… that was weird dude."

She threw her hands up and lay back on the blanket while rolling her eyes. "And I liked the rest of it too. I get what you're saying. It's just not the way I have viewed life. Things are just, I don't know, easier when you stick to the facts. I know what I know. You can't fight fact. It's comfortable here."

"You will never grow if you never feel uncomfortable."

"Actually, you will always continue to grow. Well parts of you, anyway," Benjamin quickly interjected.

"What?" She was caught off guard by his response.

"Parts of humans continue to grow almost our entire lives. So technically, no matter how comfortable an individual is they are going to continue to grow. My skull is going to continue to grow and change more than once throughout my lifetime," Benjamin explained while pointing at his head, moving his arms around his head in a circle as if he were the sun and his hands were orbiting his dome.

"And not only do we have the skull, but then you have the pelvis. This bad boy," he thrust his pelvis completely off the ground and pointed to his groin area in a rather nonsexual way, yet it still caused her to blush once again, "is going to continue to expand for…"

"All right, all right. Enough already. Jesus, Benjamin. You're going to drive me mad."

"No. You are going to drive yourself mad. Always questioning everything. Feeling you know nothing. You're so smart. Why do you say that so much?"

"None of us knows anything. It's like when you begin to convince yourself you know things, and you are certain of them, is the moment you start to become an idiot."

"Did you just call me an idiot?" He turned his head in her direction.

She turned her head to meet his eyes across the checkered blanket.

"Well... do you know?" she smirked.

"I don't even know if that was a real question you just asked. So no. I definitely know I don't know. I don't know anything right now. You confused me." Benjamin returned his glance to the clouds.

She turned her head back, looked up at the clouds, and smiled.

"No, Benjamin. I did not call you an idiot."

Silence fell upon them. A comfortable silence. The cool breeze and the sound of nature filled the air. In the three months that she had been in the city, Benjamin and she had spent many hours together. Their relationship was never more than platonic, and she really appreciated the friendship for what it was. Effortlessly their conversations would delve into the depths of their beings on a frequent basis. It made her very uncomfortable the first couple times it happened, but she had grown use to this being their standard way of being. Neither of them really knew how it happened, and they never stopped to question it or fight it... they just were.

After a long rest from talking, Benjamin's voice filled the air once again, "Hey..."

With her eyes closed, she quietly replied "Yes Benjamin?"

"The answer to your question…"

"Which one? I ask *at least* forty-two questions per hour."

"What I think love is… beyond a logical answer."

She sat up and crossed her legs, so intrigued to hear what it was he was going to say.

"Yeah? You were letting the wheels turn a little on it, eh? What do you have for me?"

"Well… honestly… love is… well, it's you, lady. I'm thinking that, well, *you* are love. I don't know what that really means *especially* right now. But… it's you, beb."

She looked back at him in shock. Benjamin sat up and for the first time, grabbed her face, pulled it in a little closer to his. He looked her in the eyes, and she couldn't help but feel nervous and overwhelmed. He pulled her in the rest of the way and for the first time, kissed her very softly and slowly. Benjamin pulled away and looked back at her with those vibrant deep blue eyes that could light up even the darkest of rooms with that charming sexy smirk of his. Her breath had just been taken away. After what felt like to her the longest thirty seconds ever, she was able to come down from that high she just experienced.

Finally she was able to speak. "Well then… wow. That just happened. I like when you let your wheels turn."

Benjamin's smirk turned into a full smile, and he laid back down. She leaned back propped up on both elbows and stared up at the blue sky lost in her mind of consistent rapid-paced thoughts and feelings. She closed her eyes, took a deep breath, and allowed herself to replay what had just happened. She didn't know how to process this. She hadn't thought about Benjamin this way at all. She oscillated between bliss and hearing herself think *What would Zai think? Do I have feelings for Benjamin?* She knew that moment had just felt right and enjoyable, but that kiss brought more confusion than clarity.

24

"So my sister is moving to the city in a couple weeks. Go figure," she said as she stuffed a spicy tuna roll soaked in soy sauce and wasabi into her mouth. She took a couple bites, swallowed, and immediately pinched the bridge of her nose hoping to alleviate the intensity of the wasabi. Her eyes teared.

While mixing the wasabi into his soy sauce, he replied, "Well don't go crying about it. That's fantastic! Another you? Just when I thought I was already the luckiest man in the world to get to share time and space with you here, I found out there will be more of your genetics in the city of New York? Oh Lord, sweet baby Jesus, you *do* exist!"

"My sister and I are a lot alike… in the sense that we share parents and some genetics but other than that I really don't know any more, Benjamin. I don't know how much I will be having her over or going out with her. I haven't seen her in years."

"Okay. That's fine. I hear what you are saying. But what I am really hearing you say right now is, 'Benjamin, I see how excited you are at the possibility of meeting my sister in the near future and I can't wait to make that idea a reality for you." He met eyes with hers as she gave him a sassy look and he shot a smirk at her. He popped another piece of his dragon roll into his mouth and closed his eyes as he savored the tastes that flooded his taste buds.

She did not have a strong reason to not get together with all of them when Veronica got to the city. The last time they saw each other, it went just fine. They just never really saw eye to eye on many views in life, and their four-year age difference kept them distant growing up as well. Before her response to the email a few months or so ago, they hadn't exchanged words in at least a year. Maybe it was just time to build their relationship. They always say sisterhood is complicated and goes through cycles, right?

"Fine. We can all go to dinner or something when she gets into town. When? I'm not sure. Originally, she was supposed to get here months ago. And I don't know what part of the city she is going to be staying in. Work is going to be paying for her apartment while she is here so she just going with the flow."

"Wow. That's an amazing perk. Who the hell does she work for?"

"National Geographic. She is coming to New York after being in Thailand for the last nine months. I can't pretend that Veronica isn't super cool and impressive."

"Yea… I can tell you are really fired up to talk about her with that flat line tonality you have there. You're super cool and impressive yourself, babe."

She observed a physical reaction to his casual drop of calling her babe. It still hit her as a surprise from time to time. Ever since their moment in Central Park, there had been an elephant growing in whatever room the two of them found themselves in. She quickly moved from her reaction and head space and brought herself back to the present to not have the elephant grow any more. She wasn't ready for that conversation.

"Thanks Benjamin," she said in an exaggerated elongated delivery. "I didn't mean to sound flatline when I said it. She really is… and I am happy for her that she is having such success and loving the profession that she has gotten herself into. Don't ask me to tell you exactly what it is that she is doing for them, because I really don't know to be honest. I mean, she's my sister. Of course, I want to see her happy and doing well. I just, I don't know. I didn't mean anything by it," she said and followed it up with tossing another spicy tuna roll into her mouth.

"I got you. No worries, I wasn't passing judgment on you. I was only teasing. Well it sounds like we will both get to learn about what it is that she is doing for National Geographic over dinner once she arrives. When is she going to be here again?"

"Not exactly sure. Within the next couple of weeks, I think. She is going to contact me and let me know when and where she will be staying when she knows. I'll keep you in the loop… maybe. If you're lucky."

He looked at her with adoration. She gave him a look back of appreciation and uncertainty.

The server came by and dropped the check. Benjamin went to grab it, but she scooped it up before he could. He gave her a look as if he was insulted.

"I don't think so! It's my turn to pick up the tab if you recall our on-going agreement, sir. This one is all mine," she said authoritatively.

"Oh, you win this time. But this is just the battle. Don't think you have won the war," he replied mischievously.

She scrunched her eyebrows and gave him a look letting him know she had no idea what he was talking about.

He shook his head softly a bit embarrassed realizing what he said made no sense at all to him either.

She threw her card in the check book, and the server took it away.

"You back to the office?"

"Yea... we are presenting this project early next week, so it's crunch time."

"How is it going by the way?"

"I think really well. You never know if the doctors are going to take well to what we come up with. They are fickle in their temperament and tools. Plus, this is all being designed for chiropractors. They are a whole breed of their own. Speaking of chiropractors, have you ever gone to one?"

"I have. And I am way overdue; it's magical. I haven't been aligned in far too long. How about you?"

"Never. I'm kind of scared to. Well, I'm sure to get a card or fifteen next week at the presentation. I'll be sure to pass them along to you," he said and winked at her.

She thanked him as she signed the check the server had silently handed to her while they were speaking.

"Have a great afternoon. I'll see you back at the apartment later," she said as she slipped back on her light jacket.

"Later," he replied as he slipped his phone back into his pocket and headed out of the restaurant.

25

*I*t had been weeks since her latest temp job with Gabrielle at Smith-Johnson's recruiting firm, and there still hadn't been any new work coming her way. She was starting to get worried that she wasn't going to have something to tell at dinner with everyone when they met up with Veronica of what she is doing for work since being here. She had put in a couple of proposals for independent work since she had been here, but they have all fallen through too.

It started to hit her, that her leap of faith always had the potential of crashing and burning with her stuck without the means to keep this lifestyle going. She had savings she could tap into if she had to, but that was for when she was old and gray, she likes to tell herself. As she felt her heartbeat beginning to race and her breathing being held more in her chest than from her diaphragm, she closed her eyes and thought back to her yoga class.

Control the breath, control the mind, control the being that is you and your life, she thought as she took three deep breaths through her nose resetting her nervous system and bringing a wash of calm over herself in the midst of the city chaos surrounding her in all directions. She was still surprised how relaxed it made her every time she did it. It wasn't long until she was back to formulating ideas of how to solve this. For the second time since being in New York, she found herself tossing out a prayer from a space of feeling a bit defeated. Looking up to the sky she said out loud "I surrender. I trust… help me please". She laughed at herself and the absurdity, took a deep breath and decided to go grab some coffee and take her mind off things for a moment.

As she was walking looking for a new coffee shop she hadn't yet been to, she had an idea come to her from what felt like out of nowhere. The idea to sign up for a free trial to one of the WeWork buildings nearby flooded into her mind. She didn't even know if that was something she could really do, but the idea came out of nowhere and presented itself quite confidently, so she went for it. She pulled up WeWork on her phone and gave the one near Union Square a call.

The receptionist answered the phone and from her voice, she imagined her to be a hip young twenty-something-year-old. She told the girl that she was a freelancer new to the city and interested in getting a membership with that them and wanted to know if she could come in and get a tour and work from the space for the day. She gladly obliged and had her set up an appointment for a tour with one of the WeWork sales team an hour from then. She did her best to not sound annoyed at the delay of the hour to get started on this mission, but she was grateful it actually worked so she forced a smile she knew could be heard through the phone and she provided her contact information.

26

She made her way over towards the building and wandered her way around Union Square a bit. Luckily, the Union Square farmers market was open. With her hands in her pockets, she slowly walked by the lavender stand breathing in deeply the calming aroma they provide. She moved on to the next stand that was selling apple cider by the cup and take-home containers. Across the way, she saw a stand with fresh apples and other fruits. She walked over and picked one apple.

"Woah, big spender here! Watch out!" the vendor said.

"Just killing time and keeping the doctor away," she said with ease as she fished in her bag for a loose single, she knew she had in there somewhere.

"Don't worry about it," the vendor replied.

She looked up in disbelief. "Are you sure?"

"Yea… I'm feeling nice today. Plus, would hate to see you end up at the doctor of my behalf."

She smiled and thanked them generously. It was only a free apple, but she would take it. Any random act of kindness, especially here in the city was a precious moment to her.

She tossed the apple in the air, caught it, and in one swift motion took the first bite. She strolled through the market aimlessly taking in the different vendors and produce. She loved farmer's markets so much; they were full of life; both the things being sold and the people who were selling them. They were always people who were about eating local and sticking to our roots... literally.

27

She was greeted on the ground level by a young man checking people in and taking their photo for their guest badge. She handed over her license which was still from Colorado and she thought, *I wonder how long I have until I need to get that changed* as she stepped in front of the small camera and smiled. She was handed her sticker and told to head to the elevator and head up to the third floor. They knew she had arrived so have a sit in the common area and someone would be out to meet her shortly. She made her way to the elevator and headed to the third floor.

The space was wonderful. She loved it from the moment she walked in. It was bright and well lit, with tall windows on her right side. There were professionals dispersed amongst the area, all involved in different activities. Some she could tell were not working at the moment and just networking, sharing with one another whatever it is they are working on, or perhaps, just talking about the latest series they are catching up on Netflix. On her left was the check-in desk that extended out further beyond she could see. There were some stools on the side closest to her for people to gather around. Across from the desk was a large counter that she noticed had a couple of baskets of snacks and also a large cake with a sign that said: *We can't eat it all. Eat me. Please. Seriously... Eat this cake.*

It was directly next to what appeared to her the tap to a kegerator. She could definitely see herself working in this space. To her right were three long tables with chairs and outlets in the middle for collaborative work space; there were approximately ten to twelve chairs per table. There were a few people dispersed around the tables with headphones engulfed in whatever it is they were working on. Right in front of her to the right of the counter of treats, coffee, and free cake, were couches that she assumed was where she was supposed to wait for the member of the sales team to give her the grand tour.

She had a seat and continued to look around the space taking it all in. She noticed on both walls by the long tables were quotes that worked together with one another. Straight ahead of her she read, *"They always say time changes things"*. She peered over her shoulder to see what the other side said, and she then read, *"But you actually have to change them yourself."* She liked this. Like really liked this. She found herself taking out her phone trying to take a picture of both sides without being obvious and being that awkward woman taking pictures of quotes on the wall. She was successful except for the one man working at the table who saw her, but it was at that moment she realized she really didn't give a fuck whether he had seen her or not.

There was a small nook of cushions behind her where two women were grouped together working on something together. To her right, she saw a small meeting space that was designed like a photo booth- a place for a silent conference center she would assume. There were two larger meeting spaces that sandwiches the "photo booth" from what she could see.

I wonder how much it costs to work in here, she thought as she patiently waited. She knew she needed to wait until she had a project and work to work on to really come utilize the space, otherwise she would be paying to just come hang out, which she really didn't hate the idea of anyway.

A woman dressed business casual started walking her way and she could tell immediately this is the woman that she had been waiting for.

"Hi, I'm Sarah! Thanks so much for waiting, we were just wrapping up a meeting. Did you have any time to check the space out while you waited?"

The woman was so energetic. She was certain she taps into the free coffee on the counter throughout the day.

"Just from where I am sitting really… but even just from here, this space is amazing."

"It really is though. Here come on, let's go have a tour around."

She and Sarah went and did a full tour of the space, getting to see an additional four office spaces, another phone booth conference call center, and a large printing area. She was fascinated by the water fountains that also had a built-in refillable water bottle feature. She had found another simple pleasure in the city.

After the tour, Sarah brought her to her office to talk about membership options. She felt a bit guilty knowing that she came here without any intention of signing up today. However, she let Sarah walk through the options, and gave the standard "I'll think about it" response that all sales people were very familiar with. Sarah was sweet with her understanding and offered her to stay in the space for the remainder of the day to get a feel for what it would be like to be a member.

She got up from her seat and gave Sarah a kind handshake. She felt awkward giving her a handshake. She wasn't sure why exactly, but she did. She put her bag over her shoulder and headed back out to the common area to find a spot at one of the long tables and dive into her proposals and applications. She decided to take a seat facing the wall that would remind her, "But you actually have to change them yourself." She opened her laptop, and then headed over the counter where she poured herself a mug of coffee and decided to help herself to a slice of the cake that was begging to be eaten. *The calories don't count when the food is desperate and begging to be eaten,* she said to herself as she cut herself a generous slice.

As she got settled into her place and sunk her fork into her slice of cake, she was truly happy in that moment. The cake was moist and baked to perfection; yellow cake with chocolate frosting, one of her favorites. She hadn't had many sweets since coming to the city which was impressive to her since she had the biggest sweet tooth ever back in Denver. Something she was happy to leave behind in the last chapter of her life. She took a couple of bites of cake, enjoying every bite slowly treating it like an experience and a mini get away from the work, and savored the sip of coffee to wash them down. She took a single deep breath and tuned back into her laptop to land herself an opportunity in the city.

28

She had been scrolling through Upwork submitting proposals for the last hour or so when she noticed someone sit across from her horizontally and set up shop. She tried to not peer over so that they could get settled into their own work dynamic. He was wearing a baseball hat, a plain long-sleeved cotton T-shirt, and a pair of dark jeans. One thing she was noticing about this space, was that she had no way of pegging anyone for what they do or who they are with, which she found intriguing and frustrating at the same time. He opened his laptop and headed over to the counter. He returned with a cup of coffee and a generous piece of cake. She liked his style.

They had been working across from one another for about forty-five minutes when she noticed, out of the corner of her eye, him push away from the table and stand in the open space behind him. He took a deep breath and stretched his arms over his head and stretched to what she could tell was his capacity. He followed this up with a couple of lunges, touching his toes, and several other stretches with deep breathing. She respected it greatly; she was even a bit jealous. She considered getting up and doing the same but decided that would just be awkward to mimic him. He might be insulted, or just weirded out. She decided to just strike up a conversation instead.

"Oh that looks wonderful," she said as he stretched overhead again.

"Oh, that it is. I feel like I have been sitting all day, I need to get the oxygen flowing again. I highly suggest it," he said with his arms over his head tilted back, making it look like it was a bit of struggle to speak.

"I'm thinking about it. I'm definitely thinking about it," she said nodding in agreement with herself on the statement.

He took one more deep breath and then made his way back to his seat, adjusting his hat as he did so. She saw his eyes shifting from left to right across his screen reading something rapidly. He was intriguing to her. She wanted to know what he does but didn't want to disrupt the intense focus he had just put into his MacBook. Luckily for her, a few moments later, he broke his focus and struck up conversation with her.

"So what are you working on?" he said slapping the tops of his fingers on the table simultaneously. He had an impressive amount of energy coming from him even while he was sitting still in one place.

"I was here for a tour. I just moved to the city about a month ago; spending some time applying to opportunities, spending time in places where maybe opportunity and I could also find each other." She immediately questioned her delivery. She hoped it didn't come off as though she was pitching that in a way for him to step up and offer her something (although she wouldn't mind if he did).

"Oh word. Well, welcome to the city. Where are you coming from?" he asked her with body language that showed her he was genuinely interested in what her response was going to be.

"I moved from Denver. Was out there for just over three years. Ever been?" she replied.

"I have. I'm a huge snowboarder. The mountains out there are dope. I have a friend that owns one of the lodges out there at the bottom of Vail. So, if you ever want the hook up out there, you let me know. I mean, you might have your own being that you lived out there. Oh sorry, I'm Andrew, by the way," he said as he extended his hand out over the table to shake her hand.

She met him halfway shaking his hand grateful for his openness and positive energy.

"You know, I actually have never snowboarded. I lived out there for three years and I never made it on to the mountain. I might have to take you up on it… but I would be spending time on the bunny trails for a while."

"We all have to start somewhere. All great journeys begin with the first step," he said with a playful wink and finger gun.

She laughed and nodded her head. "This is true, oh wise one. Anyway, how about yourself? What are you working on over there? I wasn't trying to be nosy but I couldn't help but notice you very intensely scanning your screen a little while ago."

"Okay creeper… stalk much?" he said playfully.

She liked him. He had a really fun spirit to him. She didn't get the feeling that he was hitting on her or going to at all; he was just incredibly friendly and appeared to love people. He was one of those people that people just hoped he would become their friend.

"I was reading through the latest proposal sent over from a new potential partner. I am looking to sell part of my company and merge with another to leverage both of us. And while we are both being honest, to also give myself a bit of a financial boost; the last year has been rough for us," he said, speaking very fast. She could tell he was passionate about whatever it was that he did with his company.

"Well that sounds exciting. Good luck with that. What does your company do?" she asked adjusting herself in her seat.

"We crowdfund for tech start-ups. It's pretty dope. Start-ups that have gone through the incubator process are able to apply to join our program, and if they have already received any financial backing, we look into what they are bringing to the table and if we see the potential and could leverage their platform. And then we connect them with the right people, we take them on. A couple of our latest clients have really skyrocketed which is always super exciting."

She was impressed. His response reconfirmed that there was no way to be able to peg anyone in this work space.

"That's incredible. Good for you. Congratulations! Who are some of the companies that you help leverage?"

"Yeah, thank you. It's been an amazing journey the last four years. It's incredible how something that was just an idea will actually come to fruition when we focus on it and believe it will happen. Don't get me wrong, we have had some super hard times, right now being one of those obstacles, but I'm confident the merger is going to really help us and whoever I end up decided to partner with. Hm, who are some of our bragables."

Before he could answer, she interjected "Andrew, I hope this isn't a weird response to all of that or come off strange, but I'm grateful you decided to sit across from me. You are really refreshing," she said with a relaxed genuine tone.

"Aw, aren't you sweet! I'm grateful I sat across from you too. So what kind of work are you looking for anyways? I mean obviously I can't help you directly, I am selling off half my company to keep us going and hopefully growing, but I would be lying if I said I don't know some people who know some people."

"Well, my background is in marketing. I was doing consulting work in Denver for clients in a couple of different industries. Won't lie to you and say any of them were in the tech start-up sector though," she said with a slightly defeated tonality that she didn't mean to express.

"I know it might be hard to believe, but I do have friends and know people outside of the start-up tech industry too," he said with a sarcastic twang.

She gave him a playful facial expression acknowledging his smartass intention.

"No way. Really?" she said returning his sarcasm.

"Send me your résumé, I'll see what I can do," he said while turning to the back of his chair to fish out one of his business cards from the front pocket of his REI book bag. He handed the card over the table, and she gave it a scan as she placed it down on her laptop in front of her.

"Wow, Andrew. Thank you so much. I really appreciate it."

"No promises, obviously. But sure thing, why not?" he said with a smile. "Now, leave me alone. I have proposals to read," he said with a wink while picking up his headphones and plugging them into the headphone jack.

She put her hands up with a smile. "Leaving you alone. I'll send over my résumé now and include my contact information in the email as to not disturb you any more."

"Perfect. Cheers!" he said as he put his earbuds into his ears and dived back into his illuminating screen.

One Week Later...

29

She and Zai were strolling through the market on Saturday morning. Zai had woken her up that morning by jumping into her bed and snuggling her asking her to get up and play. Her director had given them the first half of the day off from rehearsal, so she wanted to take in as much of her day as possible and didn't want to spend it alone. She gladly welcomed the morning love from Zai and agreed to peel herself out of her glorious bed as long as they didn't have to go travel anywhere far from their part of the city.

"Girl, I have the first half of the day free, as in not having to be inside. You think I want to spend anytime riding the subway today? It's Saturday, let's go to the market. Never disappoints. Get up, I'll see you out here in like, what do you say twenty minutes?"

"Not a chance. See you in thirty-five to forty," she said flatly.

"What a princess you can be. Fine. See you in thirty-five to forty minutes," Zai said as she rolled out of her bed and headed out of her room.

They made their way to the market that was only about a ten- to fifteen-minute walk from their front door. They stopped at the coffeeshop across the street and got themselves a caffeinated beverage.

"I feel like such a rebel. Being out on a Saturday morning... drinking caffeine. Dehydrating myself," Zai said with a sarcastic and enthusiastic tone. She hadn't been able to enjoy a Saturday morning in months with this production approaching. She smiled at her as she poured her almond milk into her coffee.

They crossed the street and passed the lavender tent that is always in that corner spot right across the entrance by the Starbucks. Without being prompted, they both slowed down their pace, closed their eyes and took a deep breath in as they walked by. When they opened their eyes, they looked at each other with a loving smile and interlocked arms. Zai placed her head on her shoulder, and gently touched heads. They walked intertwined with each other for the next couple of booths.

While looking through some vegetables and picking out some produce to bring back for the week, she asked Zai about her family.

"My family is pretty all right. I used to be really close with them all, but when I decided to move from Washington, they started to distance themselves emotionally. I suppose the whole distancing myself physically had something to do with it."

"Siblings?" she asked while she fondled a couple bunches of carrots deciding which ones looked most appealing to her.

"One older brother and a younger sister. Middle child syndrome. You couldn't tell with my need to be over the top expressive in everything I do?" she said with a light chuckle amused with her own quirks. "Denise lives in Northern California as a lawyer, and Xavier is still in Washington. He became a brew master and opened his own bar about four years ago. He is doing really well. Last I talked to him he is planning to open a second location in the next couple years."

"Nice. Perhaps we should go to the West Coast sometime," she said as a half empty gesture.

"Yeah... perhaps. When I'm not enslaved by directors and exhibits. It has been years since I have been back over there. I miss everyone, but we are all old now doing our own things. How about you? I know you have tons of siblings. Other than your younger sister, Vanessa, is it?"

"Veronica," she corrected her.

"Yeah, Veronica. Other than her and the kind of sort of idea of what she does as far as you know, what is the rest of your family up to?"

"Oh geez, there are a lot of us. Six total. I was the towards the top of the middle. Mom and Dad are still down in Tennessee doing their farm thing, as they will until the day they die. The estate will go to Richard if I had to guess.

He is the oldest, he is still living in Tennessee doing something with farming in some capacity. Then you have Lou and Robert who both made their way to Montana oddly enough. They launched an app together a couple of years ago that has been doing pretty well. It works with the national parks to give the best hiking trails and options for the time of year that someone is going to them. Why they chose Montana, I don't know, but that is where they are. And then you have Veronica and myself and… oh my God, who am I missing? Oh geez! What an awful sister I am, and then you have the baby of the bunch, Regina. She is finishing up her senior year at SCU. She is the rebellious wild child. I love her. I never talk to her really, but what I hear about her through my mom's bitching makes me so proud," she said with a smirk looking up and Zai.

They both laughed.

"Six siblings. I can't even imagine," Zai said as they strolled along to the next stand.

"Yea, a whole gaggle of goons. Mom and Dad weren't playing around. How about you Zai, do you want to have kids some day?"

Without hesitation, she said sharply, "Nope. Never have. Why? I don't know. I just have zero desire. Don't like hanging out with them, don't like the idea of raising one and being responsible for them. Just… no." She exhaled realizing that she answered that very strongly. With a softer tone she said, "How about yourself?"

"I do… I think. One day, maybe. My biological clock is ticking away so I don't know if it is going to be in the cards for me, but I think I want to have a little one running around one of these days", she responded while distracting herself with playing on her phone. "Oh my God!" she said as she stopped walking and paused staring down at her phone.

"What? Everything okay?"

"So last week, I went and worked at the WeWork building over on Irving for a little bit and I sat across from this really cool guy who owns a business, and he told me to pass along my résumé to him and he would see what he could do for me. So I did, but I didn't think he would actually do something with it; just thought he was being nice. He just emailed me; he has two different friends who have said they would love to schedule a time to meet with me for potential projects."

"Holy shit! That's great! See, told you that you had nothing to worry about. Everything always falls into place, especially when you are as a beautiful inside and out as you," she said interlocking arms with her and taking a step to get them to start moving again. She placed her head on Zai's shoulder. Zai gave the top of her head a kiss and they both continued to walk with a smile on their faces.

30

She was standing at the counter frozen from the news she had just received from the other end. She just landed a $80,000 contract deal with one of the companies Andrew had put her in contact with. She left their interview earlier that week unsure about how it went; she had a hard time reading the co-founders. She was to start the following Monday. She had done it. With funds still in the bank to spare. Benjamin walked into the apartment while she was still staring off into the distance wrapping her mind around how everything had fallen so perfectly into place.

"Hey there slugger… something interesting on the wall catch your eye there?" he said as he came along the side of her following where her stare was. The stare in the abyss was of nothingness but the wall.

"Oh, hey," she said looking at him out of the corner of her eye now that he had broken her daze. "No… I uh, so, I just got news from that company down in FiDi I interviewed with earlier this week. Benjamin, I got it. It's a $80,000 contracted position. I can't believe it," she said with eyes that had now watered up as the reality of this news settled in after speaking about it out loud.

"No kidding! That is amazing! I knew you would! Yes!" he picked her up in a huge hug and spun her around. In one quick motion without any thought he pulled away from her slightly while still holding her up and kissed her. They both paused in that moment and stared at one another right in the eye. There was a couple of seconds that to them both felt like eternity.

"Oh, I uh… I'm sorry. I mean I am not sorry… but," Benjamin began to stammer trying to read her and how to move forward.

"It's okay, Benjamin. I love how natural and right that felt, actually"

"Yea? It felt right to you?"

She sighed. "Yes. It felt right the first time you kissed me in the park and it feels right now. I'm scared shitless because I don't know what it means for our friendship and all of this," she exclaimed while motioning her arms to mean the entire apartment "but you really are the most amazing man I have met to date".

It was one of those pauses where they both knew what was going to happen next. Benjamin took a couple steps towards the counter, picked her up and carefully placed her down. With her legs hanging off the counter, Benjamin stood between her legs and held her face in his hands looking down at her with eyes of pure admiration. He leaned in and gave her a soft gentle kiss and then returned to where he had just been. She smiled at him, looking up into his eyes accepting that this moment has been formulating over the last months and no longer nervous or doubting it in anyway. He leaned back in to kiss her again, this time holding it longer and parting his lips softly slipping his tongue into her mouth. She kissed him back, feeling herself become weaker as she was submersed in his passion.

She slowly lifted her arms over her head, and he smoothly removed her shirt quickly replacing the cotton of her T-shirt with his lips. She opened each of Benjamin's buttons of his light blue button-down shirt while melting to the kisses along her neck and collarbone. He grabbed her around the waist and pulled her up against him. He picked her up and carried her to his bedroom kicking the door closed behind him.

31

*T*hey never left Benjamin's bedroom that night except to grab leftovers from the fridge that they shared naked under the navy sheets of Benjamin's king-sized bed and the occasional bathroom trip.

It was the next morning, and she woke up to the warmth of Benjamin's body pressed up against her backside, enclosing her in his body, making her the little spoon. She smiled and adjusted herself slightly to wiggle herself deeper into the nook he had created with the bending of his body.

At the same time, they jumped from their place of comfort as a crash from the kitchen hit their ears. It sounded like Zai had dropped a plate or mug into the sink. She turned over to Benjamin and he greeted her gaze with a smile and a kiss to the forehead.

"I would be lying if I said that I haven't pictured this moment for quite some time," he said softly with his lips still resting on her forehead.

"You really are too sweet to me sometimes."

"Oh, I'm sorry. I can start to be a dick if you want me to. Anything you wish, my lady," he said as he ran his hand along the curves of her body that was warm from the bedding and body heat.

As her body accepted his caress and her body rose with excitement following his hand, she said, "Wow, you really are able to turn on the sass at any given moment, aren't you? We haven't been awake for an hour yet. That's rather impressive Benjamin. I suppose I can work with you being sweet a bit longer," she said with a smile and pressed in him and softly bit his lip and his caress moved to grabbing her right butt cheek. He pulled her on top of him, and she sat up tall with both hands on his chest.

Looking up at her Benjamin said with a flat tone, "You seriously are so beautiful that it hurts."

His words hit her strongly and they sank into her swelling her heart full and open.

Playfully she responded with a punch to the chest and said, "Hurts like this?"

They both laughed and he flipped her on to her back now being the dominant one and said, "No hurts like this!" And began to tickle her. She let out an uncontrollable laugh that Benjamin instantly grew addicted to and refused to stop for another three minutes or so not wanting her uncontrollable laughter to ever end. Finally stopping, Benjamin rested himself on her and they both breathed deeply in sync with one another while she had her arms wrapped around his back and head.

They both looked at each other with a worrisome look when they heard a knock on the door. If Zai didn't know that she spent the night in Benjamin's room, she definitely did now since the loud laughter and hollowing coming from behind the door.

"Good morning, Zai," Benjamin called out to her while walking towards his dresser to throw on a fresh pair of boxers.

"Good morning to you both!" Zai called back through the door, "Does anyone have time to go grab breakfast before heading into work? I'm going to head out in about an hour"

Benjamin turned his head towards his bed to get a read of what his appropriate answer should be. With a tilt of her head Benjamin gave a silent response of being down for some breakfast.

She let out a soft worried sigh of Zai's disapproval and awkward energy that may creep into the apartment now, and said, "I'm in. I'll go jump in the shower real quick."

Zai said back, "Yea you better... you dirty girl," in a sassy tone and then let out a laugh.

She threw her head back and rolled out of Benjamin's bed, looking on the floor for her clothes from yesterday.

Once dressed, she walked out into the living room where Zai was standing at her desk working on some kind of drawing. She turned towards her as she came into the space, and they made eye contact and Zai just smiled. She opened her mouth unsure what to say, but Zai interjected her pause.

"It's cool girl. It's been a long time coming. I saw this shit from a mile away. Good for you guys. Just don't fuck things up and make us have to find a new roommate. Is he coming with us?" she said with a playful but assertive tone.

"I don't think so. He is still deciding," she replied as she smiled and walked towards Zai to give her hug.

Zai gave her a quick hug and said, "I'm serious, go shower with your dirty ass self. I want to go to breakfast. Don't let me get hangry."

"Oh Lord, go eat an apple. Do not let that monster come back out. The world isn't ready for that this early in the morning."

Zai gave her a light tap on the ass as she walked away from her. She put a little skip in her step and headed into the bathroom.

32

At breakfast she found herself smiling to herself and replaying the ecstasy that was shared between her and Benjamin that night. As she was smiling to herself buttering her toast, Zai asked her if she was going to share some stories and insights of how their friend and roommate is in the sack.

"Do you *really* want to know? Is this going to make this weird? As is I am still feeling weird about this for a couple of different reasons before telling you details," she responded.

With her fork full of an oversized bite of French toast to her face, Zai shook her head and decided that maybe it was best that they saved that conversation for another time and potentially never.

She did share that it was amazing and that was all that she was going to say about that.

"I knew you two were going to get together. I just knew it. I called it a while ago."

"Yeah, yeah, yeah… maybe you planted the seed with your prediction. I don't know though, Zai, we both know Benjamin is great. And I have enjoyed this evolution a lot—but I am still very nervous about the whole thing. We are roommates, I don't want to put this on us, but what if something goes sour?"

"And you think about this after you already got naked and let him bring you to orgasm?" she said with a small mouth full of French toast.

"Not even just once... multiple orgasms," she said with a bit of sassiness with her own mouthful of breakfast on her fork being waved in the air as she spoke waiting to be tossed into her mouth. "All of this has just kind of happened. I have been nervous and unsure about it the whole time. The fact that he is a great guy, we get along, and I enjoy his company has never been the part that made me unsure, so I have just been going with it. It's been making me happy so..."

"Well there you go. If it is making you happy, then shut and up and happy already," she said with a bobbing of her shoulders with her coffee mug being hugged at the center of her chest.

She sighed with a light smile, "You're right. Might as well bask in the good while the good is here, rather than ruin it with wasted energy on potential bad that doesn't even exist yet happening."

"Mm. Preach sister. Preach!" Zai said energetically with both hands up as if she was in a church praising.

"I can't wait for this production to be over, girl. This woman is in need of some sweet tender loving herself."

"Have you been dating or seeing anyone lately?" she asked after a slow sip of coffee was enjoyed.

"I went on a couple of dates with a guy a few months ago; we met at a café around the corner from the studio. The sex was awful. I couldn't do it any more. Besides, he was kind of weird. When we first met, the weird was interesting and intriguing. I was hanging around because I wanted to understand him, and I just had a lot of questions. He was like a walking mystery. But then, after some dates and spending the night a couple of times, I realized… no, no. That weirdness was just because he was really weird," she said looking off into the distance recalling some events that happened during that relationship.

They both laughed and took a couple more bites of their breakfast before putting their utensils down and throwing their napkins on top to signal to the server to come clear their plates.

"You ready to get out of here?" Zai said as she stretched over the back of her chair with her hands over her full belly.

"Yea, but I am going to head uptown. I have some errands I need to tend to."

"Oh! What are the chances you could pick up an article of clothing for me from the dry cleaners up there? I had to bring it to this specific one because they are known to be able to work with this combination of material.

"Text me the address. That shouldn't be a problem. Just need to make sure my day brings me in a path where I could get that and be coming home. Because I love you dearly, but I am not going to travel around Manhattan all day with a large costume strapped to my back or over my arm," she said kindly. She was proud that she didn't immediately oblige to the request and thought about her needs and day first.

"Oh hell no. Good call; I'll send it over to you when I get back to the apartment."

"Sounds good. I'll grab the check, get out of here."

Zai didn't fight her on it. They had grown into the routine of picking up the tab for one another thanks to Benjamin. They go out for meals together quite often, so they have the unspoken agreement that it all balances out in the long run. Zai blew her a kiss and glided out of the café with that Zai like poise and grace that she always carries.

33

A text message from a number that she did not recognize popped up on her screen while she was browsing a sample sale at one of the designer studios on Lexington.

"*Hey sis, it's Veronica. Made it into town a couple of days ago. They have me staying down near Bleeker Street on the LES. Let's figure out a time to meet up next week.*"

The time to reconnect with Veronica was approaching. She still did not know why exactly she felt so resistant and nervous about the idea, but something in her gut told her that she was not going to enjoy this experience. She stopped her browsing and stood with both feet firmly on the ground standing tall in the middle of the studio fully engulfed in her screen texting with both hands. She responded:

"Hey V, welcome, welcome. Bleeker is not too far from us, so that works out pretty nicely. What does your schedule look like?"

"Subject to change, but from what they have told me, most nights should be fine. Does Wednesday night next week work for you?"

"It should. My roommate Benjamin is going to be joining us, so let me make sure that Wednesday works for him too."

"Oh sweet, can I bring the guy I am seeing too?"

For a moment she grew agitated that Veronica had made the assumption that she was sleeping with Benjamin, but they she realized that is ridiculous since she was in fact sleeping with Benjamin. She felt more relieved than anything else at the idea of having more people joining at dinner to carry conversation, so without much hesitation beyond her unjustified kneejerk emotional response, she responded,

"Yes. Please do. I'll check with Benjamin and let you know. If it's all good on our end, want me to make the reservation?"

"Yea that would be great. We should be fine on my end; I would be the only potential conflict. As long as you don't hear something otherwise from me things are all good."

She locked her phone and slipped it back into her back pocket and began to browse through the sample rack again. She took the hanger that was holding a pair of extremely ripped denim jeans off the rack and held them out in front of her. She knew she had more than enough pairs of jeans, and this was an unnecessary purchase, but she fell in love with them. Holding them up to her to see if the length would accommodate her long legs, she smiled when she saw they match her perfectly. Hesitantly, she reached for the price tag to see how much damage to her checking account it would do. Before she panicked at the $350 price tag, she reminded herself that there is room for bargaining her with it being a sample sale. She took a deep breath and walked over the counter, getting herself into the boss lady negotiator mindset.

"These are incredible. Did you design them?" she asked the petite woman behind the counter.

"Oh God no! The designer is in London right now; I just work with her. Glad you like them; how will you be paying today?" the woman said with little enthusiasm and pushing to make the transaction a thing of the past.

She took a deep breath trying to not be obvious with her transition into negotiator in her mind. She replied as assertively as she could, "I'll give you $150 in cash for them."

"Ma'am, these are $350 jeans. That is less than half of the price of them. I think I am supposed to be insulted on behalf of the designer. Would you like to pay the $150 cash and the rest on a card? Or would you like to do all on a card today?"

That was not how she imagined that going at all. She let her wheels turn for a moment of what the next angle would be to have these jeans in her possession for far less than $350.

"Now, I know that these sample sales only last a day or so and then you're pretty much *sold* on moving these samples for profit. How about we meet at $225?"

"These prices are not negotiable. They are what they are. If you can't afford them, I'm sorry, but I think we are just going to have to let this be the end."

She was extremely insulted by her choice of words and assumption that it was her inability to buy them and not that she was smart and always looking for a bargain. It was at that moment she decided that she was not going to spend a dime in that store, and she was feeling feisty. A mixture of her lingering uncertainty with things with Benjamin and now Veronica being in town, she had many mixed emotions on several things swirling around in her body all at once. She could feel some kind of emotional overwhelmed eruption brewing underneath the surface. Some of that energy was about to be channeled into this rude young woman.

She took a deep breath with her hands up to her mouth with palms pressed together and eyes closed, gathering her thoughts and choice of words without going too overboard of what she felt was a justified expression of how she really felt.

"All right, so first of all. This is a sample sale; taking a price less than the ticket isn't unheard of. It's called being smart and making your money work for you. Maybe one day when you get a job where you start making real money you will understand that a bit more. Second, you better believe an email will be written to someone somewhere about your rude ass remark of me being unable to buy these. I could purchase multiple pairs and then another item or two for this selection without blinking an eye if I wanted to. But I will not be spending any money here and will never even look in the direction of this designer ever again. I will be sure to include that clearly in my email over to them. Do I make myself clear? Now, best of luck to you, and I hope you have a lovely, lovely day." She turned on her heel and walked quickly out of the store.

When she got out, she took a couple of steps and leaned up against the building next door. *Why the fuck was I just so mean?* she asked herself. She had never gone off on a sales associate like that. *I went way too far. I insulted her to the core of what she does for a living. Shit. I should probably go apologize.* She stood looking side to side on the street deciding if she was going to walk back in and apologize for her outburst. After some consideration, she decided that she wasn't going to and that hopefully the associate has enough esteem to not let her words shake her. After all, her words held merit. They would have just been better received if her delivery would have been kinder and with intention.

She made her way over to a tea house a couple of blocks over to get a peppermint tea and settle herself back into a calm place. It was about that time for another yoga class she decided. She pulled out ClassPass and checked to see what was available for that afternoon. Four o'clock Jivamukti Open at the Jivamukti Yoga School NYC which was right near her apartment. She wasn't familiar with Jivamukti so before booking it she decided to spend a little bit of time learning what it was. There are so many different types of yoga and found it interesting that it seemed there were different types depending on what she was needing in that moment.

She went to Google and typed in *Jivamukti* and clicked on the first link that popped up. It was to the main Jivamukti Yoga website. After scrolling through the homepage and allowing her senses to be stimulated by the soft music in the background and the visual stimulation, she navigated her way to page with the overview of the core of what Jivamukti is.

She learned that this branch of yoga is a practice that helps to improve people's relationship to all others which leads to the journey of enlightenment. When one hits enlightenment, realization of the oneness amongst all beings, the sense of separateness becomes dissolute, and one discovers long-lasting happiness. 'Sounds intense' she thought as she read through the paragraph. *Enlightenment and long-lasting happiness sounds like a pretty sweet perk. I don't know if I'm ready for this.* She continued to read and learned that their beliefs fall in the place of one's relationship to others should be mutually beneficial and come from a place of consistent joy and happiness.

She went through the class descriptions to see which would be the best for her; there were six different options. Open, Basic, Beginner Vinyasa, Spiritual Warrior, In-class private, and meditation. She knew off the bat that Spiritual Warrior was out of the picture for her that day. Her options came down to Beginner Vinyasa, Basic, meditation, and Open. She had a hard time sitting still for more than ten minutes to meditate so a full hour-long class was out of the picture. Shifting her eyes from left to right across the class descriptions screen, she decided that Open was her best bet. It was a mixed level class and included chanting, the practice, and meditation. *'Most bang for my buck'* she thought, as she booked herself a spot in the four-thirty.

34

She crossed the street from the Union Square Station and had to check the address on ClassPass again unsure if she had the right building. She walked in and took the elevator to the second floor. When it opened, she was greeted with a beautiful desk with two yogis standing behind. She found her gaze scanning the area to the left where there was a store and what appeared to be a café follow, and a long hallway that clearly led to multiple studios and amenities. She was so grateful she chose that studio out of them all. From the moment the elevator doors opened, she was having an experience.

She checked in and they offered her a towel and asked if she would like a quick tour. She happily obliged. The young woman walked around the counter and began to walk down the corridor. She pointed out the bathroom and showers, the locker room, and the washing room where she was able to put her mat after she was finished.

Oh thank God, they are clean too, she thought nodding slightly as she walked a few steps behind the woman that she never quite caught the name of. The beautiful woman with no name left her by the locker room to be able to go get changed and told her that she would be in the studio on the left-hand side.

Walking into the locker room, she checked her phone to see if she had gotten a response from Benjamin yet about dinner on Wednesday night. Nothing yet; she was hoping to be able to go into class with one less thing on her mind. *C'est la vie,* she said to herself as she lifted her T-shirt up over her head and unhooked her bra with one hand while fishing through her bag for her sports bra. She changed into her yoga pants and threw on a new form fitting tee. She looked down at her sock covered feet and wiggled her toes at herself while looking down deciding if she wanted to take them off or not. She decided to slip off the socks and threw them in the pockets of her pants that were hanging on a hook on the wall. She made her way out of the locker room and walked by the group of people waiting outside of the studio holding conversation.

She laid her mat out in the back left corner of the room, furthest away from the front and the door that she could. She wasn't comfortable being towards the front of the room. She had not embraced the idea that people are not looking at other people's mat and practices. She didn't buy it, and she knew her yoga skills were below par, especially for a studio here in Manhattan. Along the back wall were shelves of blankets, yoga blocks, straps, and a thin book with what appeared to be chants in Sanskrit and English. She grabbed a blanket, blocks, and a strap walking back towards her mat. She arranged her yoga tools and had a seat on her blanket looking forward to the alter that was put together at the front of the room.

It was stunning. It had what she believed to believe was a statue of Ganesha, surrounded with fresh flowers and a couple of other small items that she could not make out from her seat. She moved around in her seat every couple of moments, waiting for any of the others from outside in the hallway to come in and join her. After five minutes, three people who were clearly friends all walked in together places their mats in a row with one another towards the center of the room. With her feet in front of her, the bottom of her feet pressed against one another with her knees splayed to the side, she hugged her feet and bent at her waist, releasing her lower back and feeling a deep stretch through her legs and lower back.

The rest of the class trickled in over the next ten minutes, everyone settling in and either turning to speak with their mat neighbor, go into a meditative trance, or do some kind of stretch or pose. She observed a bit and found it fascinating how each person coming in had a very different way about moving into their practice. It was easy to tell everyone was coming from very different kinds of days so far. Some were clearly stressed out of their minds, seeking their mat for an escape from the world and hoping to clear the fog and chatter that hasn't stop since they got to the office this morning. Then there was the woman who was radiating inner peace and beauty. She had no idea what her day had looked like before being united in that space together, but she would place any amount of money on the bet that her day had been much more pleasant and much less stressful that the man sitting catty corner to her.

The instructor came in and introduced herself as she passed out the chanting books and said that the chant that would be followed could be found on page seven: it was the Vajrasattva mantra. She turned to page seven and under Vajrasattva's mantra she read:

Sanskrit:
oṃ vajrasattva samayam
anupālaya
vajrasattva tvenopatiṣṭha
dṛḍho me bhava
sutośyo me bhava
supośyo me bhava
anurakto me bhava
sarva siddhiṃ me prayaccha
sarva karma su ca me
cittaṃ śreyaḥ kuru hūṃ
ha ha ha ha hoḥ
bhagavan sarva tathāgatavajra
mā me muñca
vajrī bhava mahā samaya sattva
āḥ (hūṃ phaṭ)

English Translation:
Oṃ Vajrasattva! Preserve the bond!
As Vajrasattva stand before me.
Be firm for me.

Be greatly pleased for me.
Deeply nourish me.
Love me passionately.
Grant me siddhi in all things,
And in all actions make my mind most excellent.
hūṃ!
ha ha ha ha ho!
Blessed One! Vajra of all the Tathāgatas! Do not abandon me.
Be the Vajra-bearer, Being of the Great Bond!
āḥ (hūṃ phaṭ)

She had no idea how to say it in Sanskrit, but reading the English translation moved her as she finished. There were power in these words. She could feel it. She read through it one more time before putting the book down, placing her hands in her lap, and closing her eyes breathing deeply trying to find the Zen state people speak of. She was relaxed, but her mind was still having quite a few thoughts popping up and running around on her. She stayed with it and with a sound of a gong breaking her train of breath, she knew that her first Jivamukti Yoga class had begun.

35

The instructor, Cathy had a seat on her mat by the altar at the front of the room. She greeted everyone with gratitude for taking time out of their day to be present, and to create a new energy with all of their energies contributing. It was at that moment she felt slightly uncomfortable but decided to ride it out and hear more and try to come at the situation from an understanding place.

She thought about how she had just been looking at the different classmates that clearly had had very different types of days simultaneously but now, at this moment, they were all in the same place and the same time looking to achieve a similar state of being. The goal was to walk out all the same: free from anything that may have been disrupting the state of being present and free from worries. With that thought that entered her mind and exploded like a bomb went off, she smiled slightly, took a deep breath and she elongated her spine. She had known that yoga was beneficial, and it was helping; however, it was with that awakening thought, she knew that this practice was about to be her first real connection to the journey of yoga.

Cathy read through the mantra once before breaking down to them the significance of this mantra in the Tibetan practice. This one-hundred-syllable mantra is considered one of the most powerful and standard mantras to get used when a student is beginning to dive into their study and practice. The Vajrasattva's mantra is a powerful prayer that is used for purification and invokes the mainstreams of all the Buddhas. She was asked to join Cathy in reciting the chant all together. She did her best to follow along. A couple of times she said it with her eyes closed and a slight smile on her face taking in the noise and energy that was being created within and around her. After the chant they did a sound of om, and then she was asked to move to table top position and they moved on to the asana(movement) portion of the ninety-minute practice.

The physical practice was difficult for her. She found herself sweating within the first twenty minutes of the practice. Her first forward fold and down dog were difficult with the tightness of her legs still stiff despite her stretching before class.

By the time she was lying on her back moving into Shavasana, she felt her hips and legs loose and much more relaxed than she had been in weeks. After hearing Cathy's voice tell her to wiggle her toes and begin to gently make movement with her wrists and ankles. She rolled over on to her right side as she was instructed. Feeling like a content, safe, infant she lay with her eyes closed and her breath shallow. She pushed up to a seated position on Cathy's instructions, and the group moved into a ten-minute meditation practice to close the class. By the time Cathy provided them with a closing chant and abundance blessing to carry into the rest of their day, she felt like she was going to be able to float back to the apartment. She had never experienced a yoga class like this.

She felt like she was sharper in the mind, but ready to slip into the best sleep of her life. She was in love; all other yoga classes she had been to she knew were good for her, but she never felt completely different. This class was different. She felt changed. Similar to how she felt after the kundalini yoga class. She rolled up her mat allowing herself to experience the magical feeling of being completely present — something that she had always heard of but wasn't able to full grasp ever in her life.

Cathy closed out the class with a blessing and wishing of peace, a group sound of om, and a recognition of the inner light that was being reflected back to her from those on their mats, Namaste.

As people were packing up their belongings, she stayed seated breathing allowing herself to really experience and be present for what she was feeling in that moment. Cathy came over to her, introduced herself, and asked her if this was her first class. She told her that it was. She explained how she had taken a few classes with her friend who is a yogi back in Denver, and a class or two since getting here but never have really connected and committed to a yoga practice.

"Well I'm happy you found us and came to try us out. What did you think of the class?" Cathy asked with her hands naturally falling together at her heart space as she spoke.

"Cathy... is it too soon to tell you I love you?" she replied. They both laughed before she continued. "This is the first yoga class that at the end I feel completely different. I mean, you can see me now, I haven't moved yet, and I am so content just being."

"Well, you can be for another ten minutes or so before the next class comes in, so please do. But that is great. When I started my yogic journey ten years ago, I tried out a couple of different branches too. Your body and soul will align with what is best for you and the healing that is needed," Cathy said softly, speaking from the heart.

Talk like this was still a little far out to her. She wanted to believe it. It sounds great, and she could not deny that she was feeling significantly better and different after this class, but there was still a part of her that was resistant.

"I will definitely be back. That chant by the way, I don't know if I will ever be able to recite that, but once you said that it is known to be one of the powerful chants it resonated. There was a lot of power packed into that mantra."

"Indeed there was. There is so much power in words and sound. Everything is a vibration, including ourselves. When we are mindful of the words and sounds we choose, we become mindful of ourselves and where we are. Have you ever been to a sound healing ceremony before?"

"I haven't. Casey told me about one once, but it was not really my scene back then."

"My scene," Cathy recited back to her not judgementally, but with a playful tone expressing she found that use of words entertaining to her.

"Yea, maybe not the right words…"

"Oh you're fine. I'm just a word person, sometimes when a combination of words are put together, they land in a way I want to re-experience, so I say it back out loud. It's a quirk. Hope you are not offended."

"Not in the slightest," she responded with a smile.

"Beautiful. So, yes, sound healing. There is a session being put on by one of my friend's. On Thursday evening, at their studio that just opened. Are you interested?"

She was very caught off guard by this conversation. She hadn't expected to leave with an invitation to a sound healing session. However, after deciding to give Jivamukti a chance and loving how she was feeling, she decided at that moment to commit to going.

"Amazing! Way to say yes to life! That's where the magic shows up you know… in saying yes and showing up in life," Cathy said clapping her hands lightly multiple times and then standing with her hands on her hips.

She laughed a bit towards Cathy's response and walked over towards her bag that was sitting near the yoga props at the back of the room. She grabbed her phone and handed it to Cathy. "Put your number in here and I will text you so you can pass along the details."

"Totally! Well thank you for deciding to allow yourself to bask in the post yoga bliss and just be for a moment. Cheers to new friendship and another positive life altering moment to come," she said while typing her number in the phone and then handing in back to her as if it was a Champagne glass being lifted.

She finished putting Cathy in her phone as 'Cathy Yogi' as she walked back into the changing room to switch back into her high waisted business slacks and loose-fitting button down top.

She took a stroll through the shopping area that was on the other side of the yoga studio. She walked around touching the different items, she liked how everything here felt. Similar to when she walked through the apartment for the first time; she could just feel that things were right there. As she ran her hands along a row of books and then some displayed jewellery, she found herself thinking about what Cathy had said about words and everything having a vibration and wondered if that applies to non-living things and sounds too. *'I'll have to google that one later'* she thought. Standing tall with both feet firmly planted on the ground and her legs in a strong slightly open legged stance. She reached out for the book at eye level. *The Bhagavad Gita* was in her hands, and she moved it from the right to the left hand back and forth several times before stopping with it in her left hand, flipping the book over to read the back cover. It was here that she read:

In The Bhagavad Gita, *Prince Arjuna asks direct, uncompromising questions of his spiritual guide on the eve of a great battle.*

In this best-selling and expanded edition of the most famous — and popular — of Indian scriptures, Eknath Easwaran contextualizes the book culturally and historically and explains the key concepts of Hindu religious thought and the technical vocabulary of yoga.

She decided to buy it. She headed over to the counter to pay. The man behind the counter was sweet and kind. She couldn't wait to come back again and start to spend time here. After exchanging gratitude with Leo, she made her way into the café taking up the back portion of the left side of the studio. There were several couple and triples of people gathered together in numerous of conversations. She walked up to the counter and ordered a fresh pressed juice and found a seat at a small table across from the counter. She pulled out her new purchased book and flipped open to the middle of it.

36

Now hear, O son of Prtha, how by practicing yoga in full consciousness of Me, with mind attached to Me, you can know Me in full, free from doubt.

I shall now declare unto you in full this knowledge both phenomenal and noumenal, by knowing which there shall remain nothing further to be known.

Out of many thousands among men, one may endeavor for perfection, and of those who have achieved perfection, hardly one knows Me in truth.

Earth, Water, Fire, Air, Ether, Mind, Intelligence, and False Ego: all together these eight comprise My separated material energies

Besides this inferior nature, O might-armed Arjuna, there is a superior energy of Mine, which are all living entities who are struggling with material nature and are sustaining the universe…

Her focus on the page was broken by the calling out of her, Green Radiance To-Go to be picked up at the counter. She closed the book, held it to her heart quickly, and then placed it in her bag while standing and walking forward.

With her juice in hand and bag slung over her shoulder, she made her way back to the elevator feeling like a new version of herself. It was as if everything she had known up to that moment was just flipped into a new perspective allowing for her to view the world and everything in it with fresh eyes. She held the strap of her bag lying over her chest, looking down at her feet in the elevator humming softly to herself swaying to the melody she was making up as she went. She felt so light and full of love for all of life and everything. She was looking forward to her walk home and sharing time with Benjamin.

37

"A sound healing session… what the hell is that woman? What are you trying to drag me to?" Benjamin asked as he popped himself up onto the counter and took a bite out of his large red apple.

She had a feeling this conversation was going to go this way.

"It is like a yoga class, except you don't do anything but lay on your mat comfortably, and they play different sounds and tones, and it helps to balance you out and help improve wellness all around. I haven't done one yet so I can't really tell you more, but I hear great things, and I think you should just come find out with me," she said with her hands on her hips and her head tilted slightly to the side letting her assertiveness show.

Throwing his head back dramatically he let out a loud long "Fine."

"Thank you, pumpkin," she said leaning in and standing on her tippy toes to give him a kiss on the cheek.

"Yea, I'll give you pumpkin," he said as he wrapped his legs around her and pulled her into him so that she was now leaning up against the counter with her face close to his.

"You're my favorite. Do you know that?"

She paused for a moment and allowed the pleasant surprise of that statement hit her and fill her with joy. It felt so great to feel loved and appreciated again. It had been a while since she had felt that; with Mike it started off great and it was passionate, but it was not like this. Benjamin radiated love to her. He had been her friend and cheerleader since the day they met. He literally welcomed her with open arms and a warm heart, and things in her life had only been getting better since they have met.

"Moving here has been the best decision of my life, Benjamin. You… you're my favorite too," she said as she leaned in wrapping her arms around his head, giving him a long kiss and then hugging his head into her chest. They held their loving embrace for what felt like and for all they cared eternity.

He pulled away with his face still close to hers and said through his teeth, "This sound healing thing better be freaking cool."

She playfully head butted him and replied, "No promises."

He kissed her long and slow, as he slid himself off the counter bringing his feet to meet with hers, never letting their lips unlock. He picked her up and carried her to her room closing the door behind, not to return for next hour.

38

"Come on, Benjamin. We are going to be late!" she called out from the kitchen wiping down the counter from the crumbs she had just made from eating a couple of pretzels without anything underneath.

"You have been dreading this dinner since you first told me that she was coming to the city. Why do you care all of a sudden? With that being said, I'll be ready in like three minutes," he called out from his bedroom.

"Just because I do not feel like attending something, does not mean that I decide to show up late and be rude, Benjamin," she said stepping on the step to pop open the garbage can lid and threw the crumbs away brushing her hands together over the can.

"Oh well excuse me, Ms Sassy. I didn't know you had your sassy skirt on this evening," he said as he came out of the bedroom closing his door behind him. He looked dapper; he wore his navy-blue slacks with a crisp clean white button down with a stylish tan and dark brown jacket.

"You're lucky you're cute," she said walking up to him adjusting the neck line of his jacket. "I like to be punctual. I can't help it. My parents taught me that you have responsibilities in life and that every commit that you make becomes a responsibility. Each responsibility should be treated with your one hundred percent focus and with the heart too," she said gathering her phone and charger to throw into her oversized purse.

"You sure that your dad was a farmer, and not in the military?" Benjamin replied, looking through his wallet to make sure he had everything he needed before slipping it into his back pocket.

"Very funny. You should be happy that your woman is anal about being punctual. It shows responsibility, sir."

"My woman?"

"That's all you just got out of that?"

"No. I heard and got it all. That was just my favorite part," he said with a genuine smile looking at her across the counter.

She smiled back not even realizing what she had said and the impact that it had on Benjamin.

"Well good. I'm glad. Come on stud, we have a meal to be shared and possibly a story to remember and recall for many moons to come."

He put out his arm like the old royal would in asking a lady to join them to dance. She placed her arm softly over his, and then made their way out of the apartment with Benjamin flipping the lock on their way out.

39

The restaurant was one subway trip away. They walked the remaining thirteen minutes of travel necessary. Benjamin held the door for her as she walked into the Mexican restaurant.

It was a bit larger than most of the restaurants that she frequented since being here in the city. The walls were a deep yellow that usually would have bothered her, but she thought it complimented the rest of the ambiance really well. The tables were draped in dark green table cloths and had matching dark green napkins with heavy silverware laid out on the tables. There were about thirty tables in the place, and it was looking almost full, so they were glad they had called ahead and made reservations. Things were already going in her favor on this dinner — most places did not take reservations during the week, but lady luck must have been on her side.

They were brought to their table, and she was relieved to see that she had beaten Veronica and the man she is seeing. It is always easier to be the first at the table and greet the others as they arrive. They got settled in their seats, deciding to sit next to each other rather than across from each other even though they knew that it always looked awkward and made others feel slightly uncomfortable. They ordered margaritas deciding to not wait for the others to get started.

"I need to take the edge off, Benjamin. Don't judge me," she said turning to him as the waiter walked away to put in their drink orders.

"You never have to give me an excuse or talk me into a margarita, my lady. You're good. I'm happy about the decision. The aftermath of the presentation this week has been driving everyone at the office nuts. I can't wait for this one to be a thing of the past, so we can move on to the next project that drives us all nuts and we start the cycle all over again," he said nodding his head and browsing over the menu.

"I am still so excited for you that the project went so well. I mean more than half of the chiropractors were interested in learning more. That's a pretty good response, yes?"

"Yea... it's pretty good. I mean, I'll take it. I could always take more... but I'll take it. Aren't you just oh so excited to jump back into the world of offices and people and projects driving you crazy?" he said playfully looking at her with a glance from the side.

She paused for a moment, which made Benjamin even more intrigued about the next words out of her mouth. "You know... I really am. I have missed being in the office. I miss working with people and creating value. I love working. I know a lot of people complain about work... but to be honest, when I'm not doing it, I miss it. These last months have been fun getting acquainted with the city, but I am really ready to get in there and go play with the boys and girls of the city business world," she said with her spine straight. She realized she was speaking to herself more than Benjamin in that moment.

"You seriously turn me on in every single way you possibly could. You're magical woman."

She leaned in and gave him a kiss. They smiled and talked softly to themselves. She then heard a clearing of a throat, and she knew immediately that the time for a reunion had come.

40

*V*eronica stood on the opposite side of the table with her hands draped over the back of the chair looking at the couple. She was wearing a pair of classy loose-fitting low rise dark wash denim jeans with a loose-fitting stylish T-shirt. She was there alone.

"Hey there stranger," Veronica said with a smile that was slightly awkward but could be read as well- intentioned.

"Hello sister. Very long time no see," she said getting up to give her a hug. When they embraced, the sister bond kicked in and they gave each other a tight hug embracing and appreciating the love that was in that hug.

"It's good to see you, V," she said as she pulled away. "Hey where is your date…"

"Oh he is coming. He got caught up at some meeting here in the city or something. He said he shouldn't be too far behind us. Told him he has a fifteen-to-twenty-minute window before we start ordering without him though don't worry."

"No worries, we are here to enjoy each other and have fun. If he is still missing when we get hungry, we can just grab an appetizer or something, no big," Benjamin said standing from his seat to introduce himself.

Veronica looked at Benjamin and gave him a full look up and down as he stepped closer to her. Veronica had always been very big on appearances. As a kid, she was known as the one to beg and plead for the newest pair of sneakers and to go shopping. Mom and dad were not easy on us when it came to money, but somehow, Veronica did always end up getting her way. Veronica did a casual hair flip and her long brown hair swung over her shoulder resting on her back. She had a traveling photographer look to her for sure. She also had the relaxed radiant beauty that her sister carried. Benjamin and Veronica gave each other a quick hug, and everyone returned back to their seats.

The waiter came by and got Veronica's drink order, a gin and tonic with lime. She checked her phone and sent a quick text message, telling them that she just got word that her new man was on his way over now.

"You have been in the city for a whole, what, two weeks or so? How did you manage to scoop up a man serious enough to come out to dinner with family?"

"Firstly, it has never taken me too long to find a man to date who would be willing to meet my family, okay?" she said with an upswing to the second half of her sentence, sharing eye contact with Benjamin clearly trying to set the tone of her value from the start. "However, we met while in Thailand. I was there for work, and he booked himself a ticket for a vacation to get away. I was out on a Rua hang yao in the phang nga bay and he was also out on a Rua hang yao and he struck up a conversation".

Before being able to go any further, "what the hell is a rua hang yao?" was asked from across the table.

"It's a boat!" Veronica responded with a tone that flirted between excitement and condescension.

"Got it... as you were, V."

"I had to tell him to leave me alone because I was trying to get my shots, but I gave him my number. We met up at a restaurant around where we both were posted up and we ended up spending the rest of my free time in Thailand together. He has a lot of flexibility with his schedule and was able to set up some meetings in New York, so he is staying with me for now. It's all been quite magical really."

Veronica had shared this story of her meeting so excited that it seemed like she forgot where she was and who she was with. She was sharing her tale with herself more than anything.

"Wow, what a great love tale. Happy for you, V. Looking forward to meeting him."

"How about you two? How long have you been a couple? How did you meet?"

Benjamin turned to her, and they shared a look realizing this was the first time they were defined as a couple and got the opportunity to share their story of their meeting and falling for each other.

After a brief pause and a sip of her margarita, she opened her mouth slightly and said, "Well... we met the day I moved here to the city. Benjamin is my roommate."

"Shut up. No way. That's pretty great—and very risky. That is like the first rule to roommate rules, isn't it?"

"Not for us," Benjamin said flatly grabbing his drink and taking another sip.

"Touché," Veronica responded.

"And it's hard to say when we started dating. I have been crazy about her from the moment I saw her, and we became close friends pretty quickly. But your beautiful sister let me cross the line with her oh I do not know... how long ago was that my lady?"

"Oh geez, I really don't know. Must have been a month or so at least?"

"Is that it. Wow, that makes me really reflect right there," he said nudging her with his elbow.

"Aw, you guys are cute. Good for you. Just don't do anything to fuck it up and then have to figure out living things."

Unamused and irritated that Veronica even said that, she said back with a sassy tone, "Thanks for the advice. We'll do our best."

Veronica returned the sassy smile and checked her phone.

"Oh he is here. I am going to go meet him outside and bring him back."

"Sounds good. We'll be here," Benjamin said as Veronica got out of her seat and walked towards the front of the restaurant.

"Wow. She is…"

"She is Veronica. I told you. You did this Benjamin."

"Oh come on, she isn't *that* bad"

"No, it's fine. We will enjoy a meal, catch up, and call it a night. It is going to make my mother very happy to hear that I saw her face to face and can assure she is alive and well."

"She never phones home?"

"She never phones home. In her email to me she asked me to tell my mom she says hello. She has a phone and email. She has no excuse other than she can be a self-centered bitch."

"Well count your blessings. You clearly got the better genes in this competition."

"Thanks, stud," she said nudging him with her elbow and then quickly resting her head on his shoulder.

"You got it sweet cheeks," he said turning his head and giving the top of her head a quick kiss.

41

*B*enjamin and his beautiful counterpart were looking down at their menus discussing what appetizer or appetizers they were going to share this evening when she could hear the sound of Veronica's feet reapproaching the table. She looked up to give the man she had brought along at first impression scan, and as she lifted her head, she thought she was going to vomit immediately.

She closed her eyes and looked again to make sure she was not mistaken. She had not made a mistake. She did not know what to do at this moment. What is the best course of action? How does she go about processing and reacting in a timely and polite manner when she has no idea what it is that she is feeling in this moment. With her face going ghostly white, Benjamin instantly noticed, held her elbow and put one hand on her thigh leaning in concerned and said, "Babe, are you okay?"

"Yea... I uh... no. yes. Yes and no. Excuse me, I think I might be sick," she said moving out of her seat, moving around the table, and rushing to the back of the restaurant looking for the bathroom.

She hovered over the sink and grabbed on to the sides to keep herself from fainting or falling out of shock. She looked up at herself in the mirror and she looked like she had just run into a brick wall. It was what she felt like. She stared deep into her eyes, trying to talk herself out of crying or freaking out. Closing her eyes and attempting to breathe deep through her nose and out through her mouth, was not working. She was still not calming down. She looked herself back in the mirror and said to herself, *"Ya know, sometimes that breathing shit is just not going to cut it. Not when life throws something like this in your direction. Things have been going so well. Why? Why something like this? Why something like this right now?"*

Knowing that she could not stay in the bathroom for the rest of the evening, she splashed some water on her face and lightly slapped herself on the face to get it together. Frustrated with everything, she found the thoughts in her head were negative in every way. She said to herself, *Why the hell do we slap ourselves like that? That is so stupid. It doesn't work. What am I doing?* She was having a hard time snapping out of finding something wrong with every single thing. Just a few minutes ago, she was basking in how blessed and amazing this has all been.

She stood up straight and looked herself in the mirror and said, "That's enough. This is going to suck. But it is going to be okay. Everything is going to be okay. Stay classy, stay smart, stay bad fucking ass. You have an amazing man out there who is smitten with you. Go own this situation." With that, she gave two knuckle knocks to the bathroom sink and made her way out to the table where she had left everyone to figure out things for themselves.

42

The other three were sitting at the table and the awkwardness of the situation was radiating from the table. She couldn't help but wonder what the conversation was like when she left and was so thankful that she was able to get out of it by running away.

Poor Benjamin, she thought as she got back to the table. She stood next to her seat for a moment, and even though they tried not to, all three pairs of eyes instantly fell on her. She took a deep breath and slid into her seat.

"So..." Veronica broke the silence. "You two know each other."

"Yea..." she swallowed hard trying to let words formulate and come out in the proper order. "We sort of know each other. Mike and I—"

"I gave them the scoop," Mike interjected.

The four of them sat in silence for a couple of minutes. None of them knew what to do from there. The waiter arrived and asked them if they wanted to order any appetizers. He was hesitant because he could tell that his table was sharing a very awkward moment. Benjamin stepped in deciding whether the dinner was going to continue or not by ordering the two appetizer that's they had discussed splitting between them before Veronica and Mike showed up.

"Do you two want anything?" Benjamin asked quickly excited to have something to say to break the silence at least a little bit.

"Yea... I do not know what though. Let me see here," Mike said quickly scanning the menu with his finger. "We will take the firecracker shrimp and make that two orders of the fresh guacamole with chips please, thank you." He handed his menu over to the waiter with a single nod, then folded his hands on the table.

They were all in this dinner for the long haul. She was still sitting in her chair looking at her margarita tracing the rim with her middle finger. She could not get a grasp of her emotions and thoughts in this moment. Benjamin put his hand on her thigh, and she looked his way with her head still down. He leaned in a bit closer and said to her softly, "We can go if you want. I did not want to make a scene; I did not know what to do. If you want to go, let's go."

She shook her head slightly to indicate no and decided to take a deep swallow and become part of the table again.

She opened her mouth and said the first thing that came out.

"So Mike... how have you been? Happy to hear you got some traveling in."

The tonality screamed hurt, anger, and a hysterical outburst underlying the surface.

Mike cleared his throat and shifted in his seat. Veronica sat slightly taller on the edge of her seat and

Benjamin leaned back in his chair draping the one arm closest to her over the back of the chair opening his energy more directly to her attempting to comfort her without making it too obvious or making her feel even more uncomfortable.

"I did. I did get some traveling in," Mike said rolling the bottom of his beer bottle in a circle around the table. He cleared his throat again—he was just buying time before having to speak again, he did not really have anything in his throat. "After Denver, I decided to go take a couple months off and I went down to Thailand. I had always wanted to there and I had not gone yet…"

"Yes, I know," she said without any form of self-control. It just came out.

Mike sighed feeling defeated. Benjamin almost felt for the guy. He did not know this was coming. He did not think that anyone would have been able to see that coming from a mile away even if they had guessed. This was one of those scenarios that you only see in movies or read in a book somewhere.

"I do not really know what to do say to that. You asked me, so I answered." He cleared that imaginary spot in his throat again and shifted in his seat before starting to speak again. "I was down in Thailand, and I was just hanging out on the water, and I met Veronica. And things just happened. I am here for a bit and then at some point I will be heading back to Denver. That's my story," Mike said putting his arms out to the side in a surrendering of having nothing more to be able to say and unsure what the proper next step from there should be.

"Benjamin, where did you say you were from again?" Veronica interjected. Everyone at the table let out a silent expression of relief that the attention had been taken off them.

"I was born and raised in Salt Lake City, Utah."

"Home of the Mormons," Veronica bounced back to him.

"You got that right. I am one of them. Well, I was one of them. Most of my family still practices."

"No shit!" Mike said genuinely amused by this.

"Yes shit," Benjamin replied. They let out a laugh that was well welcomed. She was not able to let out a laugh herself at that moment, but she was grateful to have felt some tension leave the table.

The appetizers came out and they continued conversation about Benjamin and what it was like growing up in Utah to Mormons and Mike shared about the differences of coming from North Carolina and how the idea of Mormons was always like unicorns to them. They know they exist, just never really seen one for themselves to know that it is for real.

The conversation swayed back towards family across the table, which brought for a very interesting dynamic when the two ladies at the table were going to be able to speak on the same family, and each other.

"I would be interested to hear what you know about my family from Veronica's perspective versus what you know of the family from what I have told you, Mike. Do the stories match up?"

"I must be very honest right now in saying that I do not like or appreciate feeling targeted and bullied here."

"Bullied? Really? How old are we, Mike?"

"I did not ask for this situation, and I did not know this was going to happen. This is fucked up. Do you think I am okay with what is happening right now? You are not the only one freaking out inside and trying to be calm and collected here," Mike said back trying to keep a calm tone.

Benjamin spoke up, "Okay. Let's all breathe for a moment. Mike is right. He did not—"

"Mike is right?" she said sharply looking at Benjamin with a side eye.

"You did not let me finish. Do not start coming at me now. I am trying to help."

"I am not *coming at you,* Benjamin. I am questioning where you stand in this. I appreciate you trying to play the mediator, but we are all adults, we can have this conversation in a mature responsible manner. Right Mike?" she said looking back at Mike. When her eyes met his they were able to see the reflection of hurt, confusion, and love shining right back at them.

With a tone that was full of heart and defeat, Mike replied, "Right."

"How about we move off the topic of family all together? We all know enough about each other's upbringing at this point, yes? Surely there are plenty of other things we can talk about. How about work. What are you doing in the city now that you are here?" Veronica said, redirecting the conversation.

After finishing the last sip of her margarita and signaling to Benjamin without having to speak that she wanted another one so he should flag down the waiter the next time he sees him, she happily took this question and responded.

"I start on Monday, actually. When I got here, I was cruising on the money I had stored before getting laid off and also the final paycheck I had from my last opportunity." She shot Mike a hard glance of spite when she said that. Mike withered in his seat knowing that at some point that jab was going to come.

"Well geez, you are so lucky to have had that nest to be able to coast on that for a bit. National Geographic pays me well, but shit, not go and pick up and move to another city, New York City at that and coast for a couple of months and just see what happens well."

"Yea well, I busted my ass at my last consulting firm back in the day, so I got to reap the benefits of it now. But anyway, I am going to be working with a start-up tech company based down at the WeWork building in FiDi starting on Monday. I'll be working with their sales and marketing team. Going over their strategies, vision, and team dynamics.

"That is amazing!" Mike blurted out with genuine excitement and happiness for her.

Benjamin could not help but get slightly jealous and react to the obvious connection Mike was still feeling for her at that moment. Benjamin put his arm around her and said, "Yes, it is. But it is not surprising; she is an amazing woman," he said while pulling her closer to him. She had never felt so conflicted in her emotions as she did in that moment.

Mike was trying his hardest to not let that bother him, but he was conflicted internally as well. Ever since they had sat down for this dinner and he saw her again, he almost forgot Veronica was even there and had to remind himself or get surprised when he would turn his head and see her there or ask him something.

"Yes, she is," Mike finally responded after a few minutes of silence.

"Geez thanks. I do not mean to toot my own horn, but I think I'm quite the catch myself, Mike," Veronica said very annoyed.

Mike was caught off guard. He had not realized how much attention that he was not providing Veronica, and for the first time since sitting down was able to stop and think about how awkward and conflicted she must be feeling as well.

"Of course you are, Veronica. That's why I am with you," he said turning to her.

"Just be careful… he might decide to just get up and walk away one day, V," she said with her eyes watering trying to fight the tears that she could tell were going to come very soon.

"Really? We are going to do this now? Here?" Mike said getting angry.

"I mean, I was never given a chance to have a conversation about this when you left, so I suppose now is a good as time as ever," she said slapping the top of the table.

"Babe… are you sure you want to get into this? We can just leave?" Benjamin said trying to tread lightly.

"Benjamin, darling. I am going to ask you to stay out of this for a minute or two," she said to him with her eyes shining extra bright from the tears that illuminated her eyeballs.

"As you wish my lady. As you wish," Benjamin said adjusting his shirt and reaching for his margarita while looking for the waiter to be able to order another round. He knew they were going to need it.

43

"What do you want me to say?" Mike began. "And I just want to go on the record here saying that I wish to not have this conversation right here right now like this. I want to suggest us getting coffee or something just the two of us without our new significant others sitting right next to us. Just want to throw that out there."

"Well now that this has been presented, I would not mind hearing the story of why and how you ended up leaving your last girlfriend. From what it sounds like, you were a real douchebag. I like to think of my sister as a trustworthy source."

"Okay first of all, you are not close with your sister. You have not even spoken in over a year before this dinner. I know that—because I listen to you. And I know you two are not close because *both* of you have told me that before." Mike was being hit from so many different angles he did not know what to deflect or where to begin.

"So you did not just decide to up and leave out of nowhere, Mike? Because from what I remember that is exactly how it happened. We had sex that morning if I recall correctly actually." As soon as she said that she looked to Benjamin and apologized for including that factor. Benjamin held up his had excusing her.

"Wow. That is a whole new level of douchebag," Veronica said moving her chair away from Mike slightly.

Mike put his hands out and froze for a moment. He opened his mouth to speak a couple of times, failing to have express even a syllable. Finally after many attempts with starting and stopping, he was able to get something out.

"I was a douchebag. You are all right. It is fucked up what I did. And I…" He looked across the table right into her eyes with watery eyes to match hers. "…I am so sorry. There are so many times over these months I have said to myself that was the dumbest thing I have ever done. I contemplated reaching out so many times, but I felt the damage was done. There was no turning back. But I loved you, and I still do. You know that."

She felt a single tear run down her cheek, she hated that she knew that he still loved her. She knew that the day he left too. She could not comprehend what was happening and why it was all happening. Why now?

"You do not walk away from someone you love," she said slowly trying to fight herself from crying.

"I had to."

"You never even gave me a reason. Could you even give me a reason right now? There was nothing. We were great."

"Is there a reason to get a why at this point? You both have clearly moved on," Benjamin piped up.

"Benjamin... I know you are trying to help, and I know this must be hard for you, but I need you to stay out of this," she replied.

"I honestly do not know how much longer I can stand sitting at this table with the most awkward dynamic ever, watching the woman that I am crazy about have a heart to heart with her most recent ex who is saying that he still loves her after walking away and breaking her heart without a reason why, while he sits next to her sister that he is now dating. We sound like an episode of Jerry fucking Springer."

"I do not know how much more I can take either, guys. This is awful. Definitely wins the award for the most horrific dining experience to date for me. Mike, I do not know if I can do this any more. I need some time and space. All of you, I need some time and space. Benjamin, it was great meeting you; you seem like a really great man. Keep that up, please. Sister, it was great seeing you. I will give you a call tomorrow sometime or something. Mike, I will contact you. Please do not contact me." Veronica stood up from the table, blew her sister a kiss, and quickly made her way from the table heading towards the entrance of the restaurant.

Now, there sat Benjamin, Mike, and the woman that they both love. She was sitting composed wiping a tear that slipped out from her cheek every now and then.

"I can leave, guys. Maybe this would be best if you two were able to just talk this out."

She finally let down her stubborn wall and nodded in agreement with Benjamin. She said, "You're right. That sounds good. Don't worry about the check, I'll cover it." She looked at him lovingly and with a deep sadness behind her eyes.

"Do not be silly. I will grab the server on the way out and take care of it. Call me if you need me, but I will see you at home."

"You guys are already living together?" Mike asked disgustedly.

"He was my roommate before it got romantic," she said flatly.

"Interesting," Mike said.

"Yea… Interesting," Benjamin said condescendingly. "All right beautiful, I will see you soon. Chin up," he said leaning in and kissing the top of her head.

"Thank you, Benjamin," she said sincerely.

"Anything for you, my lady," he said as he looked around for the server. "Mike, take care of yourself," he said giving him a couple slaps on the back before heading towards the server.

44

The two of them sat at the table not saying a word for at least five minutes. Neither of them saw this situation or conversation being had today. About six months had passed since they have said a word to one another since parting ways in Denver. It had only been six months and already they both had changed so dramatically and had new chapters of their lives unfolding.

She finally broke the silence.

"Why?"

Mike opened is mouth to say something but failed again.

"I really just want to know why Mike. I do not understand. It took so much energy of mine to not let myself succumb to the idea that it was something that I did or that something was wrong with me, because I know there wasn't. I am a fucking amazing woman and…"

"You were too amazing," Mike said.

"Oh fuck off!" she said instantaneously.

"Listen, no matter what I say here, it is not going to go well. What are we looking to make happen here? If we both know that this conversation is the last that we are ever going to have, well then why don't we just spare ourselves this experience and just cut our losses now?"

"Because you do not get to do that to me twice, Michael. You do not get to walk away and leave me without answers again. We are here now. And I hate the fact that I know that you do still love me. In whatever weird sick way that is that I have no clue what it is any more. And I hate that I want to hear your why. And I hate how much I am happy that this happened." She was rambling passionately as she usually did when she let her mouth go without a filter.

Mike was caught off guard by her response. There were a lot more positive statements hidden in that response than he had anticipated.

"You're happy we are here right now? I'm happy you know I love you because I do."

She shook her head upset that she had to backtrack and explain her emotions and what she meant, even though she had no idea how to express what she was feeling because she did not know herself. She had not been in such a daze such as this since the day that Mike decided to leave, and she ended up buying a world map and throwing a dart at where they are now sitting.

"I'm happy to be able to have a second chance at this conversation. And no matter how big a douchebag you are, I am always going to love you too, Mike."

"You look great by the way," Mike said with a bit of lightness in his voice at hearing the sweet woman that he knew surface a bit.

She turned her head and looked down. "Thank you."

"And Benjamin seems like a really great guy."

"He is. Thanks. I am really lucky. Now stop bullshitting and sidetracking us, I want to know why, Mike."

He took the final sip of his drink and accidently slammed his glass on the table. A couple eating a couple of tables over, who were trying their best to not ease drop jumped and looked in their direction to make sure the evenings altercations had not grown violent.

"I started to have wandering eyes. I started to have conversations with women and found myself imagining what it would be like to date them. A couple of times I found myself flirt. And I never want to be that guy. I have never cheated on a woman, and I would like to keep that track record. It was not fair to you to stay with you, and I was starting to feel like I was not there completely. I love and respect you too much for that." Mike looked across the table looking extremely vulnerable and raw.

She sat with that response for a moment. There were feelings of relief, and a million more questions, and frustration.

She laughed.

"Are you laughing?" Mike asked insulted.

"I'm sorry, I think this is one of those laugh-or-cry situations. And I really do not want to cry any more, so this is what we get. So I appreciate that you respected me enough to not cheat on me. But to just walk away from what we were for finding some other women intriguing? Mike, that sounds like a bunch of bullshit. You couldn't just tell me you were feeling bored and have us talk about what was going on? You had to dramatically walk out of my life forever without the respect to tell me why?" A few tears fell from her cheeks. She pointed to them as they fell and said, "See. Told you. I stopped laughing, so now I cry."

They both laughed at this. It was the first moment of positive emotion they had shared together and towards each other since they sat down.

"Was it the right thing to do? No. Do I regret it? Every single day. Do I miss you? You better believe it. I want to tell you something but with Veronica in this whole mix, I do not know how this will go over, but from the sounds of things, I lost her tonight. That's karma for you though, isn't it?"

She grunted in agreement.

"Okay, about a month after we broke up"

"After you walked out on me"

Mike paused in frustration but took a breath and composed himself.

"Yes. After I walked out on you, about a month later, I came by your apartment and I was going to try to apologize, and well I did not make a plan after that. Knowing you and your will, I figured that would probably be the end of things, but that I could at least apologize and beg for another chance."

She stood in shock once again. Every time she felt as though she had just gotten a grasp on her emotions, something else would come swing at her to knock her down again.

Before she could respond, Mike kept going.

"So I showed up, and Ryan (the doorman) recognized me obviously, so he let me in, and I spoke with him for a little bit. He told me that you had moved out a week ago and you were subletting your apartment. Great call on the subletting by the way. When he told me you moved, I was in shock. My heart broke. It hit me that I had really ruined things forever and that I was a jackass and lost the best thing that had ever happened to me. So, I arranged things with the business to be able to take some time off the radar, and I booked my flight to Thailand. And then, you know the rest."

He came back? He realized he made a mistake and that he loved me? I had moved too fast for him to realize what had happened? Her mind was moving a million miles a minute.

With tears rolling down her face, she said, "Why didn't you call? We have phones. Why didn't you call? Why didn't you text?"

Mike upset himself, and hating to see her cry responded, "I won't ask you to not cry in a way like hey please stop crying, but in a way that it is killing me to see you cry especially here right now type of way."

As he said this, she realised he spoke sense.

"You're right," she said wiping some tears. "We are all paid here… let's get out of here and continue this out there somewhere," she said gathering her belongings. Mike happily took the distraction and movement. He got up and checked to make sure he had his wallet, phone, and keys. They walked out of the restaurant with their focus down, knowing that there were many looks coming their way from the surrounding tables.

45

*T*hey made their way to a small park a couple of blocks over, walking together in silence until they sat down again. This time rather than looking at each other they were side by side looking down and out.

"Why didn't you call or text me, Mike?" she said flatly.

"I don't have a good answer for you. Once Ryan told me that you had moved, I set it in my mind that it was over. I was not able to see any other solutions other way than from a hopeless mindset."

"We should never grieve from a hopeless mindset. We are all alive and blessed. When we lose things or people, we have to grieve from a place of faith that something better is on the horizon."

"God, I miss your random nuggets of wisdom that you drop so casually," he said swinging his feet back and forth. "Is it inappropriate to ask you if you miss me and think about me ever?"

"Yes, it is very inappropriate."

Mike sighed. She followed up his sigh with a "However…"

Mike turned his head in her direction.

"Of course sometimes I miss you or think of you. I would be lying to you if I said that I don't mostly curse your name after it happens because well, you broke my heart deeply, Mike. But yes, I do also find myself remembering the good times, or craving hummus. You ruined that for me by the way. I hope you know that, and you go to your grave with that on your conscious. You ruined hummus for me."

Mike laughed. "Oh. Come on! Hummus is and always will be a wonderful nutritious snack. You better stop associating me with hummus and get right on over that one."

They shared a laugh, and he nudged her with his elbow, and for a moment, they felt the synergy they once shared flow between them again. They felt it and allowed themselves to be in the moment and just enjoy the spontaneous reconnection that just occurred to them.

After a comfortable silence wore thin, Mike decided to ask some more bold questions since the last one went much better than he had expected.

"Do you think we were brought back together tonight for a reason?"

"You mean, to get back together or something?"

"Maybe. I don't know. I don't want to put words in your mouth, but this is serendipity in a crazy way, you have to agree."

"Mike... you slept with my sister. You dated my sister. I could probably get past the hummus thing. Getting through the walking out on me without providing any real reasoning for why, would be a tough one. Knowing that you have traveled with and slept with my sister… I think I have to draw a line somewhere."

"Yea… so what you are saying is that I don't have a chance?" Mike said with a playful smirk nudging her again.

"I'm really happy with Benjamin, Mike. It feels good to be able to say that confidently. I have been really unsure about it since it has started for so many different reasons. But he is a great guy, and we really like each other, and I want to ride this one out."

"He seems like a great guy. I don't blame you. He definitely wins in the nice guy category. I'm really happy to see you are doing well. My mind is still blown that we are sitting here together in New York City right now."

"Tell me about it. And thanks, Mike. I'm really glad we were able to have this conversation finally. Much needed closure."

He put his fist to his chest mimicking a knife going into his heart. He twisted the knife to finish himself off.

"Closure. Ouch. It's so final."

"It is, Mike. That it is. You asked if we this happened for a specific reason, and I think absolutely. It was to give us both the closure and for me, it helped to solidify that I am happy and in a really good place right now."

"I love you," he said blatantly looking her in the eyes with tears in his eyes.

"I love you too, Mike. I always will," she replied, standing up to give him a hug goodbye.

Mike stood up preparing to hug her for the last time.

He wrapped his arms around her and held her tight with his head nuzzled into her collarbone. They held one another for a long time, knowing that once they let go that was symbolic of them letting one another go from their lives. She could feel him crying softly into her. She too had tears coming down her cheeks. Finally Mike pulled his head from her collarbone and looked her in the face.

"I am so sorry for not treating you how you deserve. I will carry this with me for the rest of my life."

"Don't. Learn from it and do better next time. Carrying it around and looking at this with regret or remorse is just going to make anything to you do or anyone you date not nearly as enjoyable as it can be. Remember, grieve with faith. Not hopelessness," she said with her hands on each of his shoulders.

He gave a single nod and said, "I shall do my best. You are amazing."

"Thank you, Mike. You take care of yourself. Promise?" She held up her little pinky like they used to do when they were dating and wanted to secure whatever commitment they were making to each other.

He smiled and lifted his pinky and intertwined it with his. "Promise." They both kissed the tip of their thumb and brought their thumbs to touch one another over their locked fists. She softly pinched his cheek then held her hand there for a moment, taking in the image of his face one last time.

She began to walk away. After taking three steps, she paused and turned around and called out to Mike. He stopped in his tracks and turned around to hear what it is that she had to say.

"Good luck with Veronica on all of this. Just a forewarning, she can be a really huge bitch. She got that from my mother," she said with a smile.

Mike threw his head back and let out two force fake laughs, "Good to know. Thank you. Sounds like I am going to need it. Take care of yourself beautiful."

"You too, Mike."

She began walking again towards her subway stop without ever turning back to look at Mike again.

46

$\mathcal{R}$on greeted her by opening the door for her.

"Oh thank you, Ron. How are you this evening?" she asked still looking in her bag for her keys.

"Much better now that I got to see you. How are you? You okay? I don't mean to be nosey, but I know you went to dinner with Benjamin, you came back much later than him, and you both seem to be a mix of emotions."

"For someone not trying to be nosey, you sure have gathered quite a bit of information and asking rather boldly, Ron," she said with a friendly sarcastic tone.

"I am *so* sorry. You are right. Forget I said anything," Ron said upset with himself for mentioning it.

"No, Ron. It's okay, really. I appreciate you caring and asking. Everything between Benjamin and I is fine. I just had some things I had to tend to and finally release. I'd be lying if I said that I am not better now than I was just a couple hours ago," she said with a relaxed tone and smile.

"Well good! Now go get some rest. Not that you need any more beauty sleep, but just because you deserve it," Ron said maneuvering himself back around his desk.

"You're too sweet."

"I just speak truth. Goodnight."

"Goodnight, Ron," she said as she approached the bottom step and prepared to make her way up the four flights.

47

Benjamin was already in bed when she got home. She wasn't sure if she should sleep in her room tonight or if he would be expecting her to curl into bed. She walked into the kitchen and got herself a mug and filled it with filtered water from the fridge. She stood leaning against the counter staring out into the living room decompressing from the surprising events that just happened over the last couple of hours.

What she had expected to be a dinner of reconnecting with her sister, ended up being a closure with her ex. She was proud of herself on how she handled the whole thing. She could not have survived that without Benjamin. On the flip side, she thought that she would have never been in that situation at all if it were not for Benjamin. Before she could switch into annoyed, she shifted back into how happy she was to have received answers and closure from Mike.

She chugged the rest of her water and placed the mug in the sink. She headed into her bedroom and dug through her drawers until she found her 'Russel Brand is my homeboy' hoodie. She put it on with a pair of boy shorts and knee-high socks. She made her way into Benjamin's room and sat on the edge of the bed trying to get a read on whether he was sleeping or not.

She heard a low groan and Benjamin's voice saying, "Get over here," as he flipped onto his back and opened both of his arms wide across the bed. She rolled into his arms that he enclosed around her bringing them to the center of the bed.

"How did it go?" he asked with his lips resting on her forehead.

"As best as it could, really. It sucked, but I could not have asked for that to go any better. Thank you for being you, Benjamin."

"Oh please. It's nothing. Like truly, I just live and be me, it's nothing. Thank you for being you."

"Oh, it's nothing. Like truly, I just live and be me, it's nothing," she said back mocking him.

"Watch it woman!" he said poking her in her side.

"Don't start," she said through her teeth.

"Too tired to start. I just want to lie here and hold you. You okay with that, my woman?"

She smiled and nuzzled her head into his chest. "Yes. I am okay with that, my man."

48

"Let's go, we are going to be late," Benjamin called out to her as she was taking one last look at her make-up in the bathroom mirror.

"Wasn't it just a couple of days ago I was practically begging you to join me for this?"

"Listen Miss I love to be punctual, and it is something about me that you should love and appreciate…"

"All right, all right! I am coming!" she said as she twisted shut her mascara and headed out to the kitchen.

"To a sound healing session?"

"To a sound healing session!" she answered enthusiastically.

They left the apartment and jumped into an Uber making their way uptown to the studio.

49

The studio was immaculate. There was a cute café section and hanging plants everywhere. There were free samples of kombucha on a tray on a long table that greeted them in the hall. A tall friendly man approached them with bare feet and a warm heart. He asked their names and got them checked in. He directed them towards the studio space and told them to pick any space that they chose.

They entered the studio that had two rows of yoga mats lined across the walls. Each mat had a meditation pillow, a blanket, and eye mask set up on it. Benjamin waved his finger over the span of the studio signaling for her to pick a spot. She selected two mats on the left side of the room towards the front, where the set up was. There were several singing bowls, a gong, and drums, and a laptop all set up at the front of the room.

They got comfortable and let themselves lounge and relax as other people joined them in the room. Cathy walked in shortly after they settled in. She had forgotten that Cathy was the reason that she was here in the first place. She hopped up and went to give Cathy a hug. She said hello, introduced her to Benjamin, and then Cathy made her way to a different mat towards the back of the room.

The teacher leading the session for the night came in with his partner and greeted them all with gratitude for attending and introduced his partner as they got settled behind their places. He dove into a discussion on how much of an impact sound has on us. At that moment she and Cathy exchanged looks and a smile from across the room. He explained how there is a big shift happening in society where sources are tying science into the concepts of spirituality which is helping to expand the minds of many that found it difficult to resonate and believe in the concepts.

He invited them to get comfortable and allow themselves to succumb to the journey they were going to be led on through sound. There would be sounds that provided them with visuals; they might slip into a trance, recall memories, have visualizations, or maybe just feel. However, whatever it was that came to surface for them, they were to embrace it and enjoy it for the experience and what will come from it after.

As Benjamin lay back, he turned his head looking at her and said, "Well, see you on the other side."

She blew him and kiss, lay down, closed her eyes, ready to embrace whatever came her way with grace, poise, and faith.

To be continued...

The Author